D0427326

THE FOUNDING FATHER

THE FOUNDING FATHER

Diana Palmer

This Large Print edition is published by Thorndike Press®, Waterville, Maine USA and by BBC Audiobooks, Ltd, Bath, England.

Published in 2004 in the U.S. by arrangement with Harlequin Books S.A.

Published in 2004 in the U.K. by arrangement with Harlequin Enterprises II, B.V.

U.S. Hardcover 0-7862-6419-5 (Core)
U.K. Hardcover 0-7540-9602-5 (Chivers Large Print)
U.K. Softcover 0-7540-9849-4 (Camden Large Print)

All characters in this book have no existence outside the imagination of the author and have no relation whatsoever to anyone bearing the same name or names. They are not even distantly inspired by any individual known or unknown to the author, and all incidents are pure invention.

The text of this Large Print edition is unabridged.
Other aspects of the book may vary from the original edition.

Set in 16 pt. Plantin by Minnie B. Raven.

Printed in the United States on permanent paper.

British Library Cataloguing-in-Publication Data available

Library of Congress Cataloging-in-Publication Data

Palmer, Diana.
The founding father / Diana Palmer.
p. cm.
ISBN 0-7862-6419-5 (lg. print : hc : alk. paper)
1. Children of the rich — Fiction. 2. Pioneers — Fiction. 3. Texas — Fiction. 4. Large type books.
I. Title.
PS3566.A513F68 2004

2004040580

For Susan James

CHAPTER ONE

It took a lot to make Big John Jacobs nervous. He was tall, rawboned, with deep-set green eyes the color of bottle glass, and thick dark brown hair. His lean, rough face had scars left over from the War Between the States. He carried scars both inside and out. He was originally from Georgia, but he'd come to Texas just after the war. Now he lived in one of the wildest parts of southeast Texas on a ranch he'd inherited from his late uncle. He was building up the ranch frugally, heading cattle drives to Kansas and buying livestock with the proceeds. What he had was very little to show for fifteen years of hard work, but he was strong and had a good business head. He'd tripled his uncle's land holdings and bought new bulls from back East to breed with his mangy longhorns. His mother would have been proud.

He noted the deep cut on his left hand, a scar from a knife fight with one of a band of Comanches who'd raided his property for horses. John and his hired help had fought them to a standstill and put them on the run. His ranch was isolated and he had good breeding stock. Over the years he'd had to fight roaming Comanche raiders and renegades from over the Mexican border, as well as carpetbaggers. If it hadn't been for the military presence just after the war ended, courtesy of the Union Army, lawlessness would have been even worse.

John had more reason than most to hate Union officers. But in the part of Texas where his ranch was located, to the southeast of San Antonio, the peace had been kept during Reconstruction by a local commandant who was a gentleman. John had admired the Union officer, who'd caught and prosecuted a thief who stole two horses from the ranch. They were good horses, with excellent bloodlines, which John had purchased from a Kentucky thoroughbred farm. The officer, who rode a Kentucky thoroughbred of his own, understood the attachment a rancher felt to his blood stock. John had rarely been more grateful to another human being. Like John himself, the officer was fearless.

Fearless. John laughed at his own apprehension over what he was about to do. He didn't mind risking his life to save his ranch. But this was no fight with guns or knives. It was a much more civilized sort of warfare. In order to win this battle, John was going to have to venture into a world he'd never seen close up. He wasn't comfortable with high society folk. He hoped he wasn't going to embarrass himself.

He removed his dress hat and ran a big hand through his sweaty brown hair. He'd had Juana cut it before he'd left the 3J Ranch. He hoped it was conservative enough to impress old man Terrance Colby. The railroad magnate was vacationing in Sutherland Springs, not far from the 3J. The popular resort boasted over one hundred separate springs in a small area. John had ridden out there to speak to Colby, without a single idea of how he was going to go about it. He had figured the details would work themselves out if he made the trip.

He was uneasy in company. He'd had to pawn his grandfather's watch to buy the used suit and hat he was wearing. It was a gamble he was taking, a big one. Cattle were no good to anyone if they couldn't be gotten to market. Driving cattle to the railheads in Kansas was becoming ever more dangerous. In some areas, fear of Texas tick fever had caused armed blockades of farmers to deter Texas cattle from entry. If he was going to get his cattle to market, there had to be a more direct route. He needed a railroad spur close by. Colby owned a railroad. He'd just announced his intentions of expanding it to connect with San Antonio. It would be no great burden to extend a line down through Wilson County to the Jacobs' ranch. There were other ranchers in the area who also wanted the spur.

Old man Colby had a daughter, Camellia Ellen, who was unmarried and apparently unmarriageable. Local gossip said that the old man had no use for his unattractive daughter and would be happy to be rid of her. She got in the way of his mistresses. So Big John Jacobs had come a courting, to get himself a railroad . . .

It started raining just as he got to town. He cursed his foul luck, his green eyes blazing as he noted the mud his horse's hooves was throwing up and splattering onto his boots and the hem of the one good pair of pants he owned. He'd be untidy, and he couldn't afford to be. Terrance Colby was a New York aristocrat who, from what John had heard, was always impeccably dressed. He was staying at the best hotel the little resort of Sutherland Springs could boast, which was none too luxurious. Rumor was that Colby had come here on a hunting trip and was taking the waters while he was in the area.

John swung down out of the saddle half a block from the hotel Colby was staying at, hoping to have a chance to brush the mud off himself. Just as he got onto the boardwalk, a carriage drew up nearby. A young woman of no particular note climbed down out of it, caught the hem of her dress under her laced shoe, and fell face-first into a mud puddle.

Unforgivably, John laughed. He couldn't help it. The woman's companion gave him a glare, but the look he gave the woman was much more expressive.

"For God's sake, woman, can't you take two steps without tripping over your own garments?" the man asked in a high-pitched British accented voice. "Do get up. Now that we've dropped you off in town, I must go. I've an engagement for which you've already made me late. I'll call on your father later. Driver, carry on!"

The driver gave the woman and Big John a speaking look, but he did as he was instructed. John took note of the stranger, and hoped to meet him again one day.

He moved to the woman's side, and offered her an arm.

"No, no," she protested, managing to get to her feet alone. "You're much too nicely dressed to let me splatter you. Do go on, sir. I'm simply clumsy, there's no cure to be had for it, I'm afraid." She adjusted her oversized hat atop the dark bun of her hair and looked at him with miserable blue eyes in a pleasant but not very attractive face. She was slight and thin, and not the sort of woman to whom he'd ever been attracted.

"Your companion has no manners," he remarked.

"Thank you for your concern."

He tipped his hat. "It was no trouble. I wouldn't have minded being splattered. As you can see, I've already sampled the local mud."

She laughed and her animated face took on a fey quality, of which she was unaware. "Good day."

"Good day."

She moved away and he started into the barbershop to put himself to rights.

"John!" a man called from nearby. "Thought that was you," a heavyset man with a badge panted as he came up to join him. It was Deputy Marshal James Graham, who often stopped by John's ranch when he was in the area looking for fugitives.

They shook hands. "What are you doing in Sutherland Springs?" John asked him.

"I'm looking for a couple of renegades," he said. "They were hiding in Indian Territory, but I heard from a cousin of one of them that they were headed this way, trying to outrun the army. You watch your back."

"You watch yours," he retorted, opening his jacket to display the Colt .45 he always wore in a holster on a gunbelt slung across his narrow hips.

The marshal chuckled. "I heard that. Noticed you were trying to help that poor young woman out of a fix."

"Yes, poor little thing," he commented. "Nothing to look at, and of little interest to a man. Two left feet into the bargain. But it was no trouble to be kind to her. Her companion gave her no more help than the rough edge of his tongue."

"That was Sir Sydney Blythe, a hunting companion of the railroad magnate, Colby. They say the girl has a crush on him, but he has no use for her."

"Hardly surprising. He might have ended in the mud puddle," he added on a chuckle. "She's not the sort to inspire passion."

"You might be surprised. My wife is no

looker, but can she cook! Looks wear out. Cooking lasts forever. You remember that. See you around."

"You, too." John went on into the barbershop unaware of a mud-covered female standing behind the corner, trying to deal with wiping some of the mud from her heavy skirt.

She glared at the barbershop with fierce blue eyes. So he was that sort of a man, was he, pitying the poor little scrawny hen with the clumsy feet. She'd thought he was different, but he was just the same as other men. None of them looked twice at a woman unless she had a beautiful face or body.

She walked past the barbershop toward her hotel, seething with fury. She hoped that she might one day have the chance to meet that gentleman again when she was properly dressed and in her own element. It would be a shock for him, she felt certain.

A short while later John walked toward the Sutherland Springs Hotel with a confidence he didn't really feel. He was grateful for the marshal's conversation, which helped calm him. He wondered if Colby's daughter was also enamoured of the atrocious Sir Sydney, as well as that poor scrawny hen who'd been out riding with him? He wasn't certain how he would have to go about wooing such a misfit, although he had it in mind.

At thirty-five, John was more learned than many of his contemporaries, having been brought up by an educated mother who taught him Latin while they worked in the fields. Since then, he'd been educated in other ways while trying to keep himself clothed and fed. His married sister, the only other survivor of his family, had tried to get him to come and work with her husband in North Carolina on their farm, but he hadn't wanted to settle in the East. He was a man with a dream. And if a man could make himself a fortune with nothing more than hard work and self-denial, he was ready to be that man.

It seemed vaguely dishonest to take a bride for monetary reasons, and it cut to the quick to pretend an affection he didn't feel to get a rich bride. If there was an honest way to do this, he was going to find it. His one certainty was that if he married a railroad tycoon's daughter, he had a far better chance of getting a railroad to lay tracks to his ranch than if he simply asked for help. These days, nobody rushed to help a penniless rancher. Least of all a rich Northerner.

John walked into the hotel bristling with assumed self-confidence and the same faint arrogance he'd seen rich men use to get their way.

"My name is John Jacobs," he told the clerk formally. "Mr. Colby is expecting me."

That was a bald lie, but a bold one. If it worked, he could cut through a lot of time-wasting protocol.

"Uh, he is? I mean, of course, sir," the young man faltered. "Mr. Colby is in the presidential suite. It's on the second floor, at the end of the hall. You may go right up. Mr. Colby and his daughter are receiving this morning."

Receiving. Go right up. John nodded, dazed. It was easier than he'd dreamed to see one of the country's richest men!

He nodded politely at the clerk and turned to the staircase.

The suite was easy to find. He knocked on the door confidently, inwardly gritting his teeth to gear himself up for the meeting. He had no idea what he was going to give as an excuse for coming here. He didn't know what Ellen Colby looked like. Could he perhaps say that he'd seen her from afar and had fallen madly in love with her at once? That would certainly ruin his chances with her father, who would be convinced that he only wanted Ellen's money.

While he was thinking up excuses, a maid opened the door and stood back to let him inside. Belatedly he swept off his hat, hoping his forehead wasn't sweating as profusely as it felt.

"Your name, sir?" the middle-aged woman asked politely.

"John Jacobs," he told her. "I'm a local landowner," he added.

She nodded. "Please wait here."

She disappeared into another room behind a closed door. Seconds passed, while John looked around him uncomfortably, reminded by the opulence of the suite how far removed he was from the upper class.

The door opened. "Please go in, sir," the maid said respectfully, and even smiled at him.

Elated, he went into the room and stared into a pair of the coldest pale blue eyes he'd ever seen, in a face that seemed unremarkable compared to the very expensive lacy white dress worn by its owner. She had a beautiful figure, regardless of her lack of beauty. Her hair was thick and a rich dark brown, swept up into a high bun that left a roll of it all around her head. She was very poised, very elegant and totally hostile. With a start, John recognized her. She was the mud puddle swimmer from the hotel entrance.

He must not laugh, he must not . . . ! But a faint grin split his chiseled lips and his green eyes danced on her indignant features. Here was his excuse, so unexpected!

"I came to inquire about your health," he said, his voice deep and lazy. "The weather is cold, and the mud puddle was very large. . . ."

"I am . . ." She was blushing, now apparently flattered by his visit. "I am very well. Thank you!"

"What mud puddle?" came a crisp voice from the doorway. A man, shorter than John, with balding hair and dark blue eyes, dressed in an expensive suit, came into the room. "I'm Terrance Colby. Who are you?"

"John Jacobs," he introduced himself. He wasn't certain how to go on. "I own a ranch outside town . . ." he began.

"Oh, you're here about quail hunting," Colby said immediately. He smiled, to John's astonishment, and went forward to shake hands. "But I'm afraid you're a few minutes too late. I've already procured an invitation to the Four Aces Ranch to hunt antelope and quail. You know it, I expect?"

"Certainly I do, sir," John replied. And he did. That ranch was the sort John wanted desperately to own one day, a huge property with purebred cattle and horses, known all over the country — in fact, all over the world! "I'm sure you'll find the accommodations superior."

The older man eyed him curiously. "Thank you for the offer."

John nodded. "My pleasure, sir. But I had another purpose in coming. A passer-by mentioned that the young lady here was staying at this hotel. She, uh, had a bad fall on her way inside. I assisted her. I only wanted to assure myself that she was uninjured. Her companion was less than helpful," he added with honest irritation.

"Sir Sydney drove off and left me there," the woman said angrily with flashing eyes.

Colby gave her an unsympathetic glance. "If you will be clumsy and throw yourself into mud puddles, Ellen, you can expect to be ignored by any normal man."

Ellen! This unfortunate little hen was the very heiress John had come to town to woo, and he was having more good fortune than he'd dreamed! Lady Luck was tossing offerings into his path with every word he spoke.

He smiled at Ellen Colby with deliberate interest. “On the contrary, sir, I find her enchanting,” he murmured.

Colby looked at him as if he expected men with nets to storm the room.

Ellen gave him a harsh glare. She might have been flattered by the visit, but she knew a line when she heard one. Too many men had sought access to her father through her. Here was another, when she'd hoped he might like her for herself. But when had that ever happened? Disappointed, she drew herself up to her full height. “Please excuse me. I am in the middle of important work.” She lifted her chin and added deliberately, “My father's dog is having her bath.”

She turned and stalked toward a door between rooms, while John threw back his head and laughed with genuine glee.

Colby had to chuckle, himself, at his daughter's audacity. She never raised her voice, as a rule, and he'd long since come to think of her as a doormat. But this man pricked her temper and made her eyes flash.

“An interesting reaction,” he told John. “She is never rude, and I cannot remember a time when she raised her voice.”

John grinned. “A gentleman likes to

think that he has made an impression, sir," he said respectfully. "Your daughter is far more interesting with a temper than without one. To me, at least."

"You have a ranch, you said?" Colby asked.

John nodded. "A small one, but growing. I have begun to cross breeds to good effect. I have a longhorn seed bull and a small herd of Hereford cattle. I hope to raise a better sort of beef to suit Eastern tastes and ship it to market in Chicago."

The older man sized up his guest, from the worn, but still useful, shoes and suit and the wellworn gunbelt and pistol worn unobtrusively under the open jacket.

"You have a Southern accent," Colby said.

John nodded again. "I am a Georgian, by birth."

Colby actually winced.

John laughed without humor. "You know, then, what Sherman and his men did to my state."

"Slavery is against everything I believe in," Colby said. His face grew hard. "Sherman's conduct was justified."

John had to bite his tongue to keep back a sharp reply. He could feel the heat of the fire, hear his mother and sister screaming as they fell in the maelstrom of crackling flames. . . .

"You owned slaves?" Colby persisted curtly.

John gritted his teeth. "Sir, my mother and sisters and I worked on a farm outside Atlanta," he said, almost choking on memories despite the years between himself and the memory. "Only rich planters could afford slaves. My people were Irish immigrants. You might recall the signs placed at the front gates of estates in the North, which read, No Colored Or Irish Need Apply."

Colby swallowed hard. He had, indeed, seen those signs.

John seemed to grow another inch. "To answer your question, had I been a rich planter, I would have hired my labor, not bought it, for I do not feel that one man of any color has the right to own another." His green eyes flashed. "There were many other small landowners and sharecroppers like my family who paid the price for the greed and luxury of plantation owners. Sherman's army did not discriminate between the two."

"Excuse me," Colby said at once. "One of my laundresses back home had been a slave. Her arms were livid with scars from a mistress who cut her when she burned a dress she was told to iron."

"I have seen similar scars," John replied, without adding that one of the co-owners of his ranch had such unsightly scars, as well as his wife and even their eldest daughter.

"Your mother and sisters live with you?" Colby asked.

John didn't reply for a few seconds. "No, sir. Except for a married sister in North Carolina, my people are all dead."

Colby nodded, his eyes narrow and assessing. "But, then, you have done well for yourself in Texas, have you not?" He smiled.

John forced himself to return the smile and forget the insults. "I will do better, sir," he said with unshakeable confidence. "Far better."

Colby chuckled. "You remind me of myself, when I was a young man. I left home to make my fortune, and had the good sense to look toward trains as the means."

John twirled his hat in his big hands. He wanted to approach Colby about his spur, which would give him the opportunity to ship his cattle without having to take the risk of driving them north to railheads in Kansas. But that would be pushing his luck. Colby might feel that John was overstepping his place in society and being "uppity." He couldn't risk alienating Colby.

He shifted his weight. "I should go," he said absently. "I had no intention of taking up so much of your time, sir. I wanted only to offer you the freedom of my ranch for hunting, and to inquire about the health of your daughter after her unfortunate accident."

"Unfortunate accident." Colby shook his head. "She is the clumsiest woman I have ever known," he said coldly, "and I have found not one single gentleman who lasted more than a day as a suitor."

"But she is charming," John countered gallantly, his eyes dancing. "She has a sense of humor, the ability to laugh at herself, and despite her companion's rudeness, she behaved with dignity."

Colby was listening intently. "You find her . . . attractive?"

"Sir, she is the most attractive woman I have ever met," John replied without choosing his words.

Colby laughed and shook his head. "You want something," he mused. "But I'm damned if I don't find you a breath of fresh air, sir. You have style and dash."

John grinned at him. "Thank you, sir."

"I may take you up on that invitation at a later date, young man. In the meantime, I have accepted the other offer. But you could do me a favor, if you're inclined."

"Anything within my power, sir," John assured him.

"Since you find my daughter so alluring, I would like you to keep an eye on her during my absence."

"Sir, there would not be adequate chaperones at my ranch," John began quickly, seeing disaster ahead if the old man or his daughter got a glimpse of the true state of affairs at the Jacobs' ranch.

"Oh, for heaven's sake, man, I'm not proposing having her live with you in sin!" Colby burst out. "She will stay here at the hotel, and I have told her not to venture out of town. I meant only that I would like you to check on her from time to time, to make sure that she is safe. She will be on her own, except for the maid we have retained here."

"I see." John let out the breath he'd been holding. "In that case, I would be delighted. But what of her companion, Sir Sydney?" he added.

"Sir Sydney will be with me, to my cost," Colby groaned. "The man is an utter pain, but he has a tract of land that I need very badly for a new roundhouse near Chicago," he confessed. "So I must humor him, to some extent. I assure you, my daughter will not mourn his absence. She only went to drive with him at my request. She finds him repulsive."

So did John, but he didn't want to rock the boat.

"I'm glad you came, young man." Colby offered his hand, and John shook it.

"So am I, sir," he replied. "If you don't mind, I would like to take my leave of your daughter."

"Be my guest."

"Thank you."

John walked toward the open door that contained a maid, Miss Ellen Colby and a very mad wet dog of uncertain age and pedigree. It was a shaggy dog, black and white, with very long ears. It was barking pitifully and shaking soapy water everywhere.

"Oh, Miss Colby, this doggy don't want no bath," the maid wailed as she tried to right her cap.

"Never you mind, Lizzie, we're going to bathe her or die in the attempt." Ellen blew back a strand of loose hair, holding the dog down with both hands while the maid laved water on it with a cup.

"A watering trough might be a better proposition, Miss Colby," John drawled from the doorway.

His voice shocked her. She jerked her head in his direction and loosened the hold she had on the dog. In the few seconds that followed, the animal gave a yelp of pure joy, leaped out of the pan, off the table, and scattered the rugs as it clawed its way to the freedom of the parlor.

"Oh, my goodness!" Ellen yelled. "Catch her, Lizzie, before she gets to the bedroom! She'll go right up on Papa's bed, like she usually does!"

"Yes, ma'am!"

The maid ran for all she was worth. Ellen Colby put her soapy hands on her hips and glared daggers at the tall green-eyed man in the doorway.

"Now see what you've done!" Ellen raged at John.

"Me?" John's eyebrows arched. "I assure you, I meant only to say goodbye."

"You diverted my attention at a critical moment!"

He smiled slowly, liking the way her blue eyes flashed in anger. He liked the thickness of her hair. It looked very long. He wondered if she let it down at bedtime.

That thought disturbed him. He

straightened. "If your entire social life consists of bathing the dog, miss, you are missing out."

"I have a social life!"

"Falling into mud puddles?"

She grabbed up the soaking brush they'd used on the dog and considered heaving it.

John threw back his head and laughed uproariously.

"Do be quiet!" she muttered.

"You have hidden fires," he commented with delight. "Your father has asked me to keep an eye on you, Miss Colby, while he's off on his hunting trip. I find the prospect delightful."

"I can think of nothing I would enjoy less!"

"I'm quite a good companion," he assured her. "I know where birds' nests are and where flowers grow, and I can even sing and play the guitar if asked."

She hesitated, wet splotches all over her lacy dress and soap in her upswept hair. She looked at him with open curiosity. "You are wearing a gun," she pointed out. "Do you shoot people with it?"

"Only the worst sort of people," he told her. "And I have yet to shoot a woman."

"I am reassured."

"I have a cattle ranch not too far a ride

from here," he continued. "In the past, I have had infrequently to help defend my cattle from Comanche raiding parties."

"Indians!"

He laughed at her expression. "Yes. Indians. They have long since gone to live in the Indian Territory. But there are still rustlers and raiders from across the Mexican border, as well as deserting soldiers and layabouts from town hoping to steal my cattle and make a quick profit by selling them to the army."

"How do you stop them?"

"With vigilance," he said simply. "I have men who work for me on shares."

"Shares?" She frowned. "Not for wages?"

He could have bitten his tongue. He hadn't meant to let that slip out.

She knew that he'd let his guard down. She found him mysterious and charming and shrewd. But he had attractions. He was the first man she'd met who made her want to know more about him.

"I might take you for a ride in my buggy," he mused.

"I might go," she replied.

He chuckled, liking her pert response. She wasn't much to look at, truly, but she had qualities he'd yet to find in other women.

He turned to go. "I won't take the dog along," he said.

"Papa's dog goes with me everywhere," she lied, wanting to be contrary.

He glanced at her over his shoulder. "You were alone in the mud puddle, as I recall."

She glared at him.

He gave her a long, curious scrutiny. He smiled slowly. "We can discuss it at a later date. I will see you again in a day or two." He lifted his hat respectfully. "Good day, Miss Colby."

"Good day, Mr. . . . ?" It only then occurred to her that she didn't even know his name.

"John," he replied. "John Jackson Jacobs. But most people just call me 'Big John.' "

"You are rather large," she had to agree.

He grinned. "And you are rather small. But I like your spirit, Miss Colby. I like it a lot."

She sighed and her eyes began to glow faintly as they met his green ones.

He winked at her and she blushed scarlet. But before he could say anything, the maid passed him with the struggling wet dog.

"Excuse me, sir, this parcel is quite maddeningly wet," the maid grumbled as she headed toward the bowl on the table.

"So I see. Good day, ladies." He tipped his hat again, and he was gone in a jingle of spurs.

Ellen Colby looked after him with curiosity and an odd feeling of loss. Strange that a man she'd only just met could be so familiar to her, and that she could feel such joy in his presence.

Her life had been a lonely one, a life of service, helping to act as a hostess for her father and care for her grandmother. But with her grandmother off traveling, Ellen was now more of a hindrance than a help to her family, and it was no secret that her father wanted badly to see her married and off his hands.

But chance would be a fine thing, she thought. She turned back to the dog with faint sadness, wishing she were prettier.

CHAPTER TWO

John rode back to his ranch, past the new-fangled barbed wire which contained his prize longhorn bull, past the second fence that held his Hereford bull and his small herd of Hereford cows with their spring calves, to the cabin where he and his foremen's families lived together. He had hundreds of head of beef steers, but they ranged widely, free of fences, identified only by his 3J brand, burned into their thick coats. The calves had been branded in the spring.

Mary Brown was at the door, watching him approach. It was early June, and hot in south Texas. Her sweaty black hair was contained under a kerchief, and her brown eyes smiled at him. "Me and Juana washed your old clothes, Mister John," she said. "Isaac and Luis went fishing with the boys down to the river for supper, and the girls are making bread."

"Good," he said. "Do I have anything dry and pressed to put on?" he added.

Mary nodded her head. "Such as it is, Mister John. A few more holes, and no amount of sewing is gonna save you a red face in company."

"I'm working on that, Mary," he told her, chuckling. He bent to lift her youngest son, Joe, a toddler, up into his arms. "You get to growing fast, young feller, you got to help me herd cattle."

The little boy gurgled at him. John grinned at him and set him back down.

Isaac came in the back door just then, with a string of fish. "You back?" He grinned. "Any luck?"

"A lot, all of it unexpected," he told the tall, lithe black man. He glanced at Luis Rodriguez, his head vaquero, who was short and stout and also carrying a string of fish. He took Isaac's and handed both to the young boys. "You boys go clean these fish for Mary, you hear?"

"Yes, Papa," the taller black boy said. His shorter Latino companion grinned and followed him out the door.

"We have another calf missing, *señor*," Luis said irritably. "Isaac and I only came to bring the boys and the fish to the house." He pulled out his pistol and checked it. "We will go and track the calf."

"I'll go with you," John said. "Give me a minute to change."

He carried his clothing to the single

room that had a makeshift door and got out of his best clothes, leaving them hanging over a handmade chair he'd provided for Mary. He whipped his gunbelt back around his lean hips and checked his pistol. Rustlers were the bane of any rancher, but in these hard times, when a single calf meant the difference between keeping his land or losing it, he couldn't afford to let it slide.

He went back out to the men, grim-faced. "Let's do some tracking."

They found the calf, butchered. Signs around it told them it wasn't rustlers, but a couple of Indians — Comanches, in fact, judging from the broken arrow shaft and footprints they found nearby.

"Damn the luck!" John growled. "What are Comanches doing this far south? And if they're hungry, why can't they hunt rabbits or quail?"

"They all prefer buffalo, *señor*, but the herds have long gone, and game is even scarce here. That is why we had to fish for supper."

"They could go the hell back to the Indian Territory, couldn't they, instead of riding around here, harassing us poor people!" John pursed his lips thoughtfully, remembering what he'd heard in Sutherland Springs. "I wonder," he mused aloud, "if these could be the two renegades from Indian Territory being chased by the army?"

"What?" Isaac asked.

"Nothing," John said, clapping him on the shoulder affectionately. "Just thinking to myself. Let's get back to work."

The next day, he put on his good suit and went back to the Springs to check on Ellen Colby. He expected to find her reclining in her suite, or playing with her father's dog. What he did find was vaguely shocking.

Far from being in her room, Ellen was on the sidewalk with one arm around a frightened young black boy who'd apparently been knocked down by an angry man.

". . . he got in my way. He's got no business walking on the sidewalk anyway. He should be in the street. He should be dead. They should all be dead! We lost everything because of them, and then they got protected by the very army that burned down our homes! You get away from him, lady, he's not going anywhere until I teach him a lesson!"

She stuck out her chin. "I have no intention of moving, sir. If you strike him, you must strike me, also!"

John moved up onto the sidewalk. He didn't look at Ellen. His eyes were on the angry man, and they didn't waver. He didn't say a word. He simply flipped back the lapel of his jacket to disclose the holstered pistol he was carrying.

"Another one!" the angry man railed. "You damned Yankees should get the hell out of Texas and go back up north where you belong!"

"I'm from Georgia," John drawled. "But this is where I belong now."

The man was taken aback. He straightened and glared at John, his fists clenched. "You'd draw on a fellow Southerner?" he exclaimed.

"I'm partial to brown skin," John told him with a honeyed drawl. His tall, lithe figure bent just enough to make an older man nearby catch his breath. "But you do what you think you have to," he added deliberately.

"There," Ellen Colby said haughtily, helping the young man to his feet. "See what you get when you act out of ignoble motives?" she lashed at the threatening man. "A child is a child, regardless of his heritage, sir!"

"That is no child," the man said. "It is an abomination. . . ."

"I beg to disagree." The voice came from a newcomer, wearing a star on his shirt, just making his way through the small crowd. It was Deputy Marshal James Graham, well known locally because he was impartially fair. "Is there a problem, madam?" he asked Ellen, tipping his hat to her.

"That man kicked this young man off the sidewalk and attacked him," Ellen said, glaring daggers at the antagonist. "I interfered and Mr. Jacobs came along in time to prevent any further violence."

"Are you all right, son?" the marshal asked the young boy, who was open-mouthed at his unexpected defense.

"Uh, yes, sir. I ain't hurt," he stammered.

Ellen Colby took a coin from her purse and placed it in the young man's hand. "You go get yourself a stick of peppermint," she told him.

He looked at the coin and grinned. "Thank you kindly, miss, but I'll buy my mama a sack of flour instead. Thank you, too," he told the marshal and John Jacobs, before he cut his losses and rushed down the sidewalk.

Graham turned to the man who'd started the trouble. "I don't like troublemakers," he said in a voice curt with command. "If I see you again, in a similar situation, I'll lock you up. That's a promise."

The man spat onto the ground and gave all three of the boy's defenders a cold glare before he turned and stomped off in the opposite direction.

"I'm obliged to both of you," Ellen Colby told them.

John shrugged. "It was no bother."

The deputy marshal chuckled. "A Georgian defending a black boy." He shook his head. "I am astonished."

John laughed. "I have a former slave family working with me," he explained. His face tautened. "If you could see the scars they carry, even the children, you might understand my position even better."

The deputy nodded. "I do understand. If you have any further trouble," he told Ellen, "I am at your service." He tipped his hat and went back to his horse.

"You are a man of parts, Mr. Jacobs," Ellen told John, her blue eyes soft and approving. "Thank you for your help."

He shrugged. "I was thinking of Isaac's oldest boy who died in Georgia," he confessed, moving closer as the crowd melted away. "Isaac is my wrangler," he added. "His first son was beaten to death by an overseer just before the end of the war."

She stood staring up into his lean, hard face with utter curiosity. "I understood that all Southerners hated colored people."

"Most of us common Southerners were in the fields working right beside them," John said coldly. "We were little more than slaves ourselves, while the rich lived in luxury and turned a blind eye to the abuse."

"I had no idea," she said hesitantly.

"Very few northern people do," he said flatly. "Yet there was a county in Georgia that flew the Union flag all through the war, and every attempt by the confederacy to press-gang them into the army was met with open resistance. They ran away and the army got tired of going back to get them again and again." He chuckled at her surprise. "I will tell you all about it over tea, if you like."

She blushed. "I would like that very much, Mr. Jacobs."

He offered his arm. She placed her small hand in the crook of his elbow and let him escort her into the hotel's immaculate dining room. He wondered if he should have told Graham about the Comanche tracks he'd found on his place. He made a note to mention it to the man when he next saw him.

Ellen liked the lithe, rawboned man who sat across from her sipping tea and eating tea cakes as if he were born to high society. But she knew that he wasn't. He still had rough edges, but even those were endearing. She couldn't forget the image she had of him, standing in front of the frightened boy, daring the attacker to try again. He was brave. She admired courage.

"Did you really come to see my father to inquire about my welfare?" she asked after they'd discussed the war.

He looked up at her, surprised by her boldness. He put his teacup down. "No," he said honestly.

She laughed self-consciously. "Forgive me, but I knew that wasn't the real reason. I appreciate your honesty."

He leaned back in his chair and studied her without pretense. His green gaze slid over her plain face, down to the faint thrust of her breasts under the green and white striped bodice of her dress and up to the wealth of dark hair piled atop her head. "Lies come hard to me," he told her.

"Shall I be completely honest about my motives and risk alienating you?"

She smiled. "Please do. I have lost count of the men who pretended to admire me only as a means to my father's wealth. I much prefer an open approach."

"I inherited a very small holding from my uncle, who died some time ago." He toyed with the teacup. "I have worked for wages in the past, to buy more land and cattle. But just recently I've started to experiment with crossing breeds. I am raising a new sort of beef steer with which I hope to tempt the eastern population's hunger for range-fed beef." His eyes lifted to hers. "It's a long, slow process to drive cattle to a railhead up in Kansas, fraught with danger and risk, more now than ever since the fear of Texas fever in cattle has caused so much resistance to be placed in the path of the cattle drives. My finances are so tight now that the loss of a single calf is a major setback to me."

She was interested. "You have a plan."

He smiled. "I have a plan. I want to bring a railroad to this area of south Texas. More precisely, I want a spur to run to my ranch, so that I can ship cattle to Chicago without having to drive them to Kansas first."

Her eyes brightened. "Then you had no real purpose of inviting my father to hunt quail on your ranch."

"Miss Colby," he said heavily, "my two foremen and their families live with me in a one-room cabin. It looks all right at a distance, but close up, it's very primitive. It is a pretend mansion. As I am a pretend aristocrat." He gestured at his suit coat. "I used the last of my ready cash to disguise myself and I came into town because I had heard that your father was here, and that he had a marriageable daughter." His expression became self-mocking when she blinked. "But I'm not enough of a scoundrel to pretend an affection I do not feel." He studied her quietly, toying with a spoon beside his cup and saucer. "So let me make you a business proposition. Marry me and let your father give us a railroad spur as a wedding present."

She gulped, swallowed a mouthful of hot tea, sat back and expelled a shocked breath. "Sir, you are blunt!"

"Ma'am, I am honest," he replied. He leaned forward quickly and fixed her with his green eyes. "Listen to me. I have little more than land and prospects. But I have a good head for business, and I know cattle. Given the opportunity, I will build an empire such as Texas has never seen. I have good help, and I've learned much about raising cattle from them. Marry me."

"And . . . what would I obtain from such a liaison?" she stammered.

"Freedom."

"Excuse me?"

"Your father cares for you, I think, but he treats you as a liability. That gentleman," he spat the word, "who was escorting you stood idly by when you fell in a mud puddle and didn't even offer a hand. You are undervalued."

She laughed nervously. "And I would not be, if I married a poor stranger and went to live in the wilds where rustlers raid?"

He grinned. "You could wear pants and learn to ride a horse and herd cattle," he said, tempting her. "I would even teach you to brand cattle and shoot a gun."

Her whole demeanor changed. She just stared at him for a minute. "I have spent my entire life under the care of my mother's mother, having lost my own mother when I was only a child. My grandmother Greene believes that a lady should never soil her hands in any way. She insists on absolute decorum in all situations. She would not hear of my learning to ride a horse or shoot a gun because such things are only for men. I have lived in a cage all my life." Her blue eyes began to gleam. "I should love to be a tomboy!"

He laughed. "Then marry me."

She hesitated once again. "Sir, I know very little of men. Having been sheltered in all ways, I am uneasy with the thought of . . . with having a stranger . . . with being . . ."

He held up a hand. "I offer you a marriage of friends. In truth, anything more would require a miracle, as there is no privacy where I live. We are all under the single roof. And," he added, "my foremen and their families are black and Mexican, not white." He watched for her reactions. "So, as you can see, there is a further difficulty in regard to public opinion hereabouts."

She clasped her hands before her on the table. "I would like to think about it a little. Not because of any prejudice," she added quickly, and smiled. "But because I would like to know you a little better. I have a friend who married in haste at the age of fifteen. She is now twenty-four, as I am. She has seven living children and her husband treats her like property. It is not a condition which I envy her."

"I understand," he said.

The oddest thing, was that she thought he really did understand. He was a complex man. She had a sudden vision of him years down the road, in an elegant suit, in an elegant setting. He had potential. She'd never met anyone like him.

She sighed. "But my father must not know the entire truth," she cautioned. "He has prejudices, and he would not willingly let me go to a man he considered a social inferior."

His thin lips pursed amusedly. "Then I'll do my utmost to convince him that I am actually the illegitimate grandson of an Irish earl."

She leaned forward. "Are there Irish earls?"

He shrugged. "I have no idea. But, then, he probably has no idea, either." His eyes twinkled.

She laughed delightedly. It changed her face, her eyes, her whole look. She was pretty when she laughed.

"There is one more complication," he said in a half-serious tone.

"Which is?"

His smile was outrageous. "We have lots of mud puddles at the ranch."

"Oh, you!" she exclaimed, reaching for the teapot.

"If you throw it, the morning papers will have a more interesting front page."

"Will it? And what would you do?" she challenged brightly.

"I am uncivilized," he informed her. "I would put you across my knee and paddle your backside, after which I would toss you over my shoulder and carry you home with me."

"How very exciting!" she exclaimed. "I have never done anything especially outrageous. I think I might like being the object of a scandal!"

He beamed. "Tempting," he proclaimed. "But I have great plans and no desire to start tongues wagging. Yet."

"Very well. I'll restrain my less civilized impulses for the time being."

He lifted his teacup and toasted her. "To unholy alliances," he teased.

She lifted hers as well. "And madcap plots!"

They clicked teacups together and drank deeply.

It was unseemly for them to be seen going out of town alone, so Ellen was prevented from visiting John's ranch. But he took her to church on Sunday — a new habit that he felt obliged to acquire — and promenading along the sidewalk after a leisurely lunch in the hotel.

The following week, John was a frequent visitor. He and Ellen became friends with an elegant Scottish gentleman and his wife who were staying at the hotel and taking the waters, while they toured the American West.

"It is a grand country," the Scotsman, Robert Maxwell, told Ellen and John. "Edith and I have been longing to ride out into the country, but we are told that it is dangerous."

"It is," John assured him grimly. "My partners and I have been tracking rustlers all week," he added, to Ellen's surprise, because he hadn't told her. "There are dangerous men in these parts, and we have rustlers from across the border, also."

"Do you have Red Indians?" Maxwell exclaimed. His eyes twinkled. "I would like to meet one."

"They're all in the Indian Territory now, and no, you wouldn't like to meet one," John said. "The Comanches who used to live hereabouts didn't encourage foreign visitors, and they had a well-deserved reputation for opposing any people who tried to invade their land."

"Their land?" the Scotsman queried, curiously.

"Their land," John said firmly. "They roamed this country long before the first white man set foot here. They intermarried with the Mexican population. . . ."

Maxwell seemed very confused, as he interrupted, "Surely there were no people here at all when you arrived," he said.

"Perhaps they don't know it back East, but Texas was part of Mexico just a few decades back," John informed him. "That's why we went to war with Mexico, because Texas wanted independence from it. Our brave boys died in the Alamo in San Antonio, and at Goliad and San Jacinto, to bring Texas into the union. But the Mexican boys fought to keep from losing their territory, is how they saw it. They considered us invaders."

Ellen was watching John covertly, with quiet admiration.

"Ah, now I understand," the Scot chuckled. "It's like us and England. We've been fighting centuries to govern ourselves, like the Irish. But the British are stubborn folk."

"So are Texans," John chuckled.

"I don't suppose you'd go riding with us, young man?" Maxwell asked him wistfully. "We should love to see a little of the area, and I see that you wear a great pistol at your hip. I assume you can shoot any two-legged threats to our safety."

John glanced at Ellen and saw such appreciation in her blue eyes that he lost his train of thought for a few seconds.

Finally he blinked and darted his green gaze back to the foreigners, hoping his heartbeat wasn't audible.

"I think I'd like that," John replied, "as long as Ellen comes with us."

"Your young lady," the Scotswoman, Nell Maxwell, added with a gentle, indulgent smile.

"Yes," John said, his eyes going back to Ellen's involuntarily. "My young lady."

Ellen blushed red and lowered her eyes, which caused the foreign couple to laugh charmingly. She was so excited that she forgot her father's admonition that she was not to leave the hotel and go out of town. In fact, when she recalled it, she simply ignored it.

They rented a surrey and John helped Ellen into the back seat before he climbed up nimbly beside her. He noted that it was the best surrey the stable had, with fringe hanging all the way around, and the horses' livery was silver and black leather.

"I suppose this is nothing special for

you," John murmured to her, looking keenly at the horses' adornments, "but it's something of a treat for me."

Ellen smoothed the skirt of her nice blue suit with its black piping. "It's a treat for me, too," she confessed. "I had very much wanted to drive out in the country, but my father only thinks of hunting, not sight-seeing, and he dislikes my company."

"I like your company very much," John said in a deep, soft tone.

She looked up at him, surprised by the warmth in his deep voice. She was lost in the sudden intensity of his green eyes under the wide brim of his dress hat. She felt her whole world shift in the slow delight it provoked.

He smiled, feeling as if he could fly all of a sudden. Impulsively his big, lean hand caught hers on the seat between them and curled her small fingers into it.

She caught her breath, entranced.

"Are you two young people comfortable?" Maxwell asked.

"Quite comfortable, thank you, sir," John replied, and he looked at Ellen with possession.

"So am I, thank you," Ellen managed through her tight throat.

"We'll away, then," Maxwell said with a

grin at his wife, and he flicked the reins.

The surrey bounded forward, the horses obviously well chosen for their task, because the ride was as smooth as silk.

"Which way shall we go?" Maxwell asked.

"Just follow the road you're on," John told him. "I know this way best. It runs past my own land up to Quail Run, the next little town along the road. I can show you the ruins of a log cabin where a white woman and her Comanche husband held off a company of soldiers a few years back. He was a renegade. She was a widow with a young son, and expecting another when her husband was killed by a robber. Soon after, the Comanche was part of a war party that encountered a company of soldiers trailing them. He was wounded and she found him and nursed him back to health. It was winter. She couldn't hunt or fish, or chop wood, and she had no family at all. He undertook her support. They both ran from the soldiers, up into the Indian Territory. She's there now, people say. Nobody knows where he is."

"What a fascinating story!" Maxwell exclaimed. "Is it true?"

"From what I hear, it is," John replied.

"What a courageous young woman," Ellen murmured.

"To have contact with a Red Indian, she would have to be," Mrs. Maxwell replied. "I have heard many people speak of Indians. None of what they say is good."

"I think all people are good and bad," Ellen ventured. "I have never thought heritage should decide which is which."

John chuckled and squeezed her hand. "We think alike."

The Maxwells exchanged a complicated look and laughed, too.

The log cabin was pointed out. It was nothing much to look at. There was a well tucked into high grass and briar bushes, and a single tree in what must once have been the front yard.

"What sort of tree is that?" Mrs. Maxwell asked. "What an odd shape."

"It's a chinaberry tree," John recalled. "We have them in Georgia, where I'm from. My sisters and I used to throw the green berries that grow on them back and forth, playing." He became somber.

"You have family back in Georgia?" Ellen asked pointedly, softly.

He sighed. "I have a married sister in North Carolina. No one else."

Ellen knew there was more to it than just that, and she had a feeling the war had cost him more than his home. She stroked the back of his callused hand gently. "Mama died of typhoid when I was just five. So except for Papa and Grandmother, I have no one, either."

He caught his breath. He hadn't thought about her circumstances, her family, her background. All he'd known was that she was rich. He began to see her with different eyes.

"I'm sorry, about your family," she said quietly.

He sighed. He didn't look at her. Memories tore at his heart. He looked out beyond the horses drawing the surrey at the yellow sand of the dirt road, leading to the slightly rolling land ahead. The familiar *clop-clop* of the horses' hooves and the faint creak of leather and wood and the swishing sound of the rolling wheels seemed very loud in the silence that followed. The dust came up into the carriage, but they were all used to it, since dirt roads were somewhat universal. The boards that made the seats of the surrey were hard on the backside during a long trip, but not less comfortable than the saddle of a horse, John supposed.

"Do you ride at all?" he asked Ellen.

"I was never allowed to," she confessed.

"My grandmother thought it wasn't lady-like."

"I ride to the hounds," Mrs. Maxwell said, eavesdropping, and turned to face them with a grin. "My father himself put me on my first horse when I was no more than a girl. I rode sidesaddle, of course, but I could outdistance any man I met on a horse. Well, except for Robert," she conceded, with an affectionate look at her husband. "We raced and I lost. Then and there, I determined that I needed to marry him."

"And she did," he added with a chuckle, darting a look over his broad shoulder. "Her father told me I must keep her occupied to keep her happy, so I turned the stables over to her."

"Quite a revolution of sorts in our part of the country, I must add," Mrs. Maxwell confessed. "But the lads finally learned who had the whip hand, and now they do what I say."

"We have the finest stable around," Maxwell agreed. "We haven't lost a race yet."

"When I have more horses, you must come and teach my partners how to train them," John told Mrs. Maxwell.

"And didn't I tell you that people would

not be stuffy and arrogant here in Texas?" she asked her husband.

"I must agree, they are not."

"Well, two of them, at least," John murmured dryly. "There," he said suddenly, pointing out across a grassy pasture. "That is my land."

All three heads turned. In the distance was the big cabin, surrounded by pecan and oak trees and not very visible. But around it were red-and-white-coated cattle, grazing in between barbed wire fences.

"It is fenced!" Maxwell exclaimed.

"Fencing is what keeps the outlaws out and my cattle in," John said, used to defending his fences. "Many people dislike this new barbed wire, but it is the most economical way to contain my herds. And I don't have a great deal of capital to work with."

"You are an honest man," Maxwell said. "You did not have to admit such a thing to a stranger."

"It is because you are a stranger that I can do it," John said amusedly. "I would never admit to being poor around my own countrymen. A man has his pride. However, I intend to be the richest landowner hereabouts in a few years. So you must plan to come back to Texas. I can promise you will be very welcome as houseguests."

"If I am able, I will," Maxwell agreed. "So we must keep in touch."

"Indeed we must. We will trade addresses before you leave town. But for now," John added, "make a left turn at this next crossroads, and I will show you a mill, where we take our corn to be ground into meal."

"We have mills at home, but I should like to see yours," Mrs. Maxwell enthused.

"And so you shall," John promised.

CHAPTER THREE

Two hours later, tired and thirsty, the tourists returned to the livery stable to return the horses and surrey.

"It has been a pleasure," John told the Maxwells, shaking hands.

"And for me, as well," Ellen added.

The older couple smiled indulgently. "We leave for New York in the morning," Maxwell said regretfully, "and then we sail to Scotland. It has been a pleasure to meet you both, although I wish we could have done so sooner."

"Yes," Mrs. Maxwell said solemnly. "How sad to make friends just as we must say goodbye to them."

"We will keep in touch," John said.

"Indeed we will. You must leave your address for us at the desk, and we will leave ours for you," Maxwell told John. "When you have made your fortune, I hope very much to return with my wife to visit you both."

Ellen flushed, because she had a sudden vivid picture of herself with John and several children on a grand estate. John was seeing the same picture. He grinned broadly. "We will look forward to it," he said to them both.

The Maxwells went up to their rooms and John stopped with Ellen at the foot of the stairs, because it would have been unseemly for a gentleman to accompany a lady all the way to her bedroom.

He took her hand in his and held it firmly. "I enjoyed today," he said. "Even in company, you are unique."

"As you are." She smiled up at him from a radiant face surrounded by wisps of loose dark hair that had escaped her bun and the hatpins that held on her wide-brimmed hat.

"We must make sure that we build a proper empire," he teased, "so that the Maxwells can come back to visit."

"I shall do my utmost to assist you," she replied with teasing eyes.

He chuckled. "I have no doubt of that."

"I will see you tomorrow?" she fished.

"Indeed you will. It will be in the afternoon, though," he added regretfully. "I must help move cattle into a new pasture first. It is very dry and we must shift them closer to water."

"Good evening, then," she said gently.

"Good evening." He lifted her hand to his lips in a gesture he'd learned in polite company during his travels.

It had a giddy effect on Ellen. She blushed and laughed nervously and almost stumbled over her own feet going up the staircase.

"Oh, dear," she said, righting herself.

"Not to worry," John assured her, hat in hand, green eyes brimming with mirth. "See?" He looked around his feet and back up at her. "No mud puddles!"

She gave him an exasperated, but amused, look, and went quickly up the staircase. When she made the landing, he was still there, watching.

John and Ellen saw each other daily for a week, during which they grew closer. Ellen waited for John in the hotel dining room late the next Friday afternoon, but to her dismay, it was not John who walked directly to her table. It was her father, home unexpectedly early. Nor was he smiling.

He pulled out a chair and sat down, motioning imperiously to a waiter, from whom he ordered coffee and nothing else.

"You are home early," Ellen stammered.

"I am home to prevent a scandal!" he replied curtly. "I've had word from an acquaintance of Sir Sydney's that you were seen flagrantly defying my instructions that you should stay in this hotel during my absence! You have been riding, in the country, alone, with Mr. Jacobs! How dare you create a scandal here!"

The Ellen of only a week ago would have bowed her head meekly and agreed never to disobey him again. But her association with John Jacobs had already stiffened her backbone. He had offered her a new life, a free life, away from the endless social conventions and rules of conduct that kept her father so occupied.

She lifted her eyebrows with hauteur. "And what business of Sir Sydney's friend is my behavior?" she wanted to know.

Her father's eyes widened in surprise. "I beg your pardon?"

"I have no intention of being coupled with Sir Sydney in any way whatsoever," she informed him. "In fact, the man is repulsive and ill-mannered."

It was a rare hint of rebellion, one of just a few he had ever seen in Ellen. He just stared at her, confused and amused, all at once.

"It would seem that your acquaintance with Mr. Jacobs is corrupting you."

"I intend to be further corrupted," she

replied coolly. "He has asked me to marry him."

"Child, that is out of the question," he said sharply.

She held up a dainty hand. "I am no child," she informed him, blue eyes flashing. "I am a woman grown. Most of my friends are married with families of their own. I am a spinster, an encumbrance to hear you tell it, of a sort whom men do not rush to escort. I am neither pretty nor accomplished . . ."

"You are quite wealthy," he inserted bluntly. "Which is, no doubt, why Mr. Jacobs finds you so attractive."

In fact, it was a railroad spur, not money, that John wanted, but she wasn't ready to tell her father that. Let him think what he liked. She knew that John Jacobs found her attractive. It gave her confidence to stand up to her parent for the first time in memory.

"You may disinherit me whenever you like," she said easily, sipping coffee with a steady hand. Her eyes twinkled. "I promise you, it will make no difference to him. He is the sort of man who builds empires from nothing more than hard work and determination. In time, his fortune will rival yours, I daresay."

Terrance Colby was listening now, not blustering. "You are considering his proposal."

She nodded, smiling. "He has painted me a delightful picture of muddy roads, kitchen gardens, heavy labor, cooking over open fires and branding cattle." She chuckled. "In fact, he has offered to let me help him brand cattle in the fall when his second crop of calves drop."

Terrance caught his breath. He waited to speak until the waiter brought his coffee. He glowered after the retreating figure. "I should have asked for a teacup of whiskey instead," he muttered to himself. His eyes went back to his daughter's face. "Brand cattle?"

She nodded. "Ride horses, shoot a gun . . . he offered to teach me no end of disgusting and socially unacceptable forms of recreation."

He sat back with an expulsion of breath. "I could have him arrested."

"For what?" she replied.

He was disconcerted by the question. "I haven't decided yet. Corrupting a minor," he ventured.

"I am far beyond the age of consent, Father," she reminded him. She sipped coffee again. "You may disinherit me at will. I will not even need the elegant wardrobes you have purchased for me. I will wear dungarees and high-heeled boots."

His look of horror was now all-consuming. "You will not! Remember your place, Ellen!"

Her eyes narrowed. "My place is what I say it is. I am not property, to be sold or bartered for material gain!"

He was formulating a reply when the sound of heavy footfalls disturbed him into looking up. John Jacobs was standing just to his side, wearing his working gear, including that sinister revolver slung low in a holster slanted across his lean hips.

"Ah," Colby said curtly. "The villain of the piece!"

"I am no villain," John replied tersely. He glanced at Ellen with budding feelings of protectiveness. She looked flushed and angry. "Certainly, I have never given Ellen such pain as that I see now on her face." He looked back at Colby with a cold glare.

Colby began to be impressed. This steely young man was not impressed by either his wealth or position when Ellen was distressed.

"Do you intend to call me out?" he asked John.

The younger man glanced again at Ellen.

"It would be high folly to kill the father of my prospective bride," he said finally. "Of course, I don't have to kill you," he added, pursing his lips and giving Colby's shoulder a quiet scrutiny. "I could simply wing you."

Colby's gaze went to that worn pistol butt. "Do you know how to shoot that hog leg?"

"I could give you references," John drawled. "Or a demonstration, if you prefer."

Colby actually laughed. "I imagine you could. Stop bristling like an angry dog and sit down, Mr. Jacobs. I have ridden hard to get here, thinking my daughter was about to be seduced by a bounder. And I find only an honest suitor who would fight even her own father to protect her. I am quite impressed. Do sit down," he emphasized. "That gentleman by the window looks fit to jump through it. He has not taken his eyes off your gun since you approached me!"

John's hard face broke into a sheepish grin. He pulled out a chair and sat down close to Ellen, his green eyes soft now and possessive as they sketched her flushed, happy face. He smiled at her, tenderly.

Colby ordered coffee for John as well

and then sat back to study the determined young man.

"She said you wish to teach her to shoot a gun and brand cattle," Colby began.

"If she wants to, yes," John replied. "I assume you would object . . . ?"

Colby chuckled. "My grandmother shot a gun and once chased a would-be robber down the streets of a North Carolina town with it. She was a local legend."

"You never told me!" Ellen exclaimed.

He grimaced. "Your mother was very straitlaced, Ellen, like your grandmother Greene," he said. "She wanted no image of my unconventional mother to tempt you into indiscretion." He pursed his lips and chuckled. "Apparently blood will out, as they say." He looked at her with kind eyes. "You have been pampered all your life. Nothing that money could buy has ever been beyond your pocket. It will not be such a life with this man," he indicated John. "Not for a few years, at least," he added with a chuckle. "You remind me of myself, Mr. Jacobs. I did not inherit my wealth. I worked as a farm laborer in my youth," he added, shocking his daughter. "I mucked out stables and slopped hogs for a rich man in our small North Carolina town. There were eight of us children, and no money to be handed down. When I was twelve, I jumped on a freight train and was arrested in New York when I was found in a stock car. I was taken to the manager's office where the owner of the railroad had chanced to venture on a matter of business. I was rude and arrogant, but he must have seen something in me that impressed him. He had a wife, but no children. He took me home with him, had his wife clean me up and dress me properly, and I became his adoptive child. When he died, he left the business to me. By then, I was more than capable of running it."

"Father!" Ellen exclaimed. "You never spoke of your parents. I had no idea . . . !"

"My parents died of typhoid soon after I left the farm," he confessed. "My brothers and sisters were taken in by cousins. When I made my own fortune, I made sure that they were provided for."

"You wanted a son," she said sorrowfully, "to inherit what you had. And all you got was me."

"Your mother died giving birth to a stillborn son," he confessed. "You were told that she died of a fever, which is partially correct. I felt that you were too young for the whole truth. And your maternal grandmother was horrified when I thought to tell you. Grandmother Greene is very correct and formal." He sighed. "When she knows what you have done, I expect she will be here on the next train to save you, along with however many grandsons she can convince to accompany her."

She nodded slowly, feeling nervous. "She is formidable."

"I wouldn't mind a son, but I do like little girls," John said with a warm smile. "I won't mind if we have daughters."

She flushed, embarrassed.

"Let us speak first of marriage, if you please," Colby said with a wry smile. "What would you like for a wedding present, Mr. Jacobs?"

John was overwhelmed. He hesitated.

"*We* would like a spur line run down to *our* ranch," Ellen said for him, with a wicked grin. "So that we don't have to drive our cattle all the way to Kansas to get them shipped to Chicago. We are going to raise extraordinary beef."

John sighed. "Indeed we are," he nodded, watching her with delight.

"That may take some little time," Colby mused. "What would you like in the meantime?"

"A sidesaddle rig for Ellen, so that she

can be comfortable in the saddle," John said surprisingly.

"I do not want a sidesaddle," she informed him curtly. "I intend to ride astride, as I have seen other women do since I came here."

"I have never seen a woman ride in such a manner!" Colby exploded.

"She's thinking of Tess Wallace," John confessed. "She's the wife of old man Tick Wallace, who owns the stagecoach line here. She drives the team and even rides shotgun sometimes. He's twenty years older than she is, but nobody doubts what they feel for each other. She's crazy for him."

"An unconventional woman," Colby muttered.

"As I intend to become. You may give me away at the wedding, and it must be a small, intimate one, and very soon," she added. "I do not wish my husband embarrassed by a gathering of snobby aristocrats."

Her father's jaw dropped. "But the suddenness of the wedding . . . !"

"I am sorry, Father, but it will be my wedding, and I feel I have a right to ask for what I wish," Ellen said stubbornly. "I have done nothing wrong, so I have nothing to fear. Besides," she added logically, "none of our friends live here, or are in attendance here at the Springs."

Her father sighed. "As you wish, my dear," he said finally, and his real affection for her was evident in the smile he gave her.

John was tremendously impressed, not only by her show of spirit, but by her consideration for him. He was getting quite a bargain, he thought. Then he stopped to ask himself what she was getting, save for a hard life that would age her prematurely, maybe even kill her. He began to frown.

"It will be a harder life than you realize now," John said abruptly, and with a scowl. "We have no conveniences at all. . . ."

"I am not afraid of hard work," Ellen interrupted.

John and Colby exchanged concerned glances. They both knew deprivation intimately. Ellen had never been without a maid or the most luxurious accommodations in her entire life.

"I'll spare you as much as I can," John said after a minute. "But most empires operate sparsely at first."

"I will learn to cook," Ellen said with a chuckle.

"Can you clean a game hen?" her father wanted to know.

She didn't waver. "I can learn."

"Can you haul water from the river and hoe in a garden?" her father persisted. "Because I have no doubt that you will have to do it."

"There will be men to do the lifting," John promised him. "And we will take excellent care of her, sir."

Her father hesitated, but Ellen's face was stiff with determination. She wasn't backing down an inch.

"Very well," he said on a heavy breath. "But if it becomes too much for you, I want to know," he added firmly. "You must promise that, or I cannot sanction your wedding."

"I promise," she said at once, knowing that she would never go to him for help.

He relaxed a little. "Then I will give you a wedding present that will not make your prospective bridegroom chafe too much," he continued. "I'll open an account for you both at the mercantile store. You will need dry goods to furnish your home."

"Oh, Father, thank you!" Ellen exclaimed.

John chuckled. "Thank you, indeed. Ellen will be grateful, but I'll consider it a loan."

"Of course, my boy," Colby replied complacently.

John knew the man didn't believe him. But he was capable of building an empire, even if he was the only one at the table who knew it at that moment. He reached over to shake hands with the older man.

"Within ten years," he told Colby, "we will entertain you in the style to which you are accustomed."

Colby nodded, but he still had reservations. He only hoped he wasn't doing Ellen a disservice. And he still had to explain this to her maternal grandmother, who was going to have a heart attack when she knew what he'd let Ellen do.

But all he said to the couple was, "We shall see."

They were married by a justice of the peace, with Terrance Colby and the minister's wife as witnesses. Colby had found a logical reason for the haste of the wedding, pleading his forthcoming trip home and Ellen's refusal to leave Sutherland Springs. The minister, an easygoing, romantic man, was willing to defy convention for a good cause. Colby congratulated John, kissed Ellen, and led them to a buckboard which he'd already had filled with enough provisions to last a month. He'd even included a treadle sewing machine, cloth for dresses and the sewing notions that went with them. Nor had he forgotten Ellen's precious knitting needles and wool yarn, with which she whiled away quiet evenings.

"Father, thank you very much!" Ellen exclaimed when she saw the rig.

"Thank you very much, indeed," John added with a handshake. "I shall take excellent care of her," he promised.

"I'm sure you'll do your best," Colby replied, but he was worried, and it showed.

Ellen kissed him. "You must not be concerned for me," she said firmly, her blue eyes full of censure. "You think I am a lily, but I mean to prove to you that I am like a cactus flower, able to bloom in the most unlikely places."

He kissed her cheek. "If you ever need me . . ."

"I do know where to send a telegram," she interrupted, and chuckled. "Have a safe trip home."

"I will have your trunks sent out before I leave town," he added.

John helped Ellen into the buckboard in the lacy white dress and veil she'd worn for her wedding, and he climbed up beside her in the only good suit he owned. They were an odd couple, he thought. And considering the shock she was likely to get when she saw where she must live, it would only get worse. He felt guilty for what he was doing. He prayed that the ends would justify the means. He had promised little, and she had asked for nothing. But many couples had started with even less and made a go of their marriages. He meant to keep Ellen happy, whatever it took.

Ellen Jacobs's first glimpse of her future home would have been enough to discourage many a young woman from getting out of the buckboard. The shade trees shaded a large, rough log cabin with only one door and a single window and a chimney. Nearby were cactus plants and brush. But there were tiny pink climbing roses in full bloom, and John confessed that he'd brought the bushes here from Georgia planted in a syrup can. The roses delighted her, and made the wilderness look less wild.

Outside the cabin stood a Mexican couple and a black couple, surrounded by children of all ages. They stared and looked very nervous as John helped Ellen down out of the buckboard.

She had rarely interacted with people of color, except as servants in the homes she had visited most of her life. It was new, and rather exciting, to live among them.

"I am Ellen Colby," she introduced herself, and then colored. "I do beg your pardon! I am Ellen Jacobs!"

She laughed, and then they laughed as well.

"We're pleased to meet you, *señora,*" the Mexican man said, holding his broad sombrero in front of him. He grinned as he introduced himself and his small family. "I am Luis Rodriguez. This is my family — my wife Juana, my son Alvaro and my daughters Juanita, Elena and Lupita." They all nodded and smiled.

"And I am Mary Brown," the black woman said gently. "My husband is Isaac. These are my boys, Ben, the oldest, and Joe, the youngest, and my little girl Libby, who is the middle child. We are glad to have you here."

"I am glad to be here," Ellen said.

"But right now, you need to get into some comfortable clothing, Mrs. Jacobs," Mary said. "Come along in. You men go to work and leave us to our own chores," she said, shooing them off.

"Mary, I can't work in these!" John exclaimed defensively.

She reached into a box and pulled out a freshly ironed shirt and patched pants.

"You go off behind a tree and put those on, and I'll do my best to chase the moths out of this box so's I can put your suit in it. And mind you don't get red mud in this shirt!"

"Yes, ma'am," he said with a sheepish grin. "See you later, Ellen."

Mary shut the door on him, grinning widely at Ellen. "He is a good man," she told Ellen in all seriousness as she produced the best dress she had and offered it to Ellen.

"No," Ellen said gently, smiling. "I thank you very much for the offer of your dress, but I not only brought a cotton dress of my own — I have brought bolts of fabric and a sewing machine."

There were looks of unadulterated pleasure on all the feminine faces. "New . . . fabric?" Mary asked haltingly.

"Sewing machine?" her daughter exclaimed.

"In the buckboard," Ellen assured them with a grin.

They vanished like summer mist, out the door. Ellen followed behind them, still laughing at their delight. She'd done the right thing, it seemed — rather, her father had. She might have thought of it first if she'd had the opportunity.

The women and girls went wild over the material, tearing it out of its brown paper wrapping without even bothering to cut the string that held it.

"Alvaro, you and Ben get this sewing machine and Mrs. Jacobs's suitcase into the house right this minute! Girls, bring the notions and the fabric! I'll get the coffee and sugar, but Ben will have to come back for the lard bucket and the flour sack."

"Yes, ma'am," they echoed, and burst out laughing.

Three hours later, Ellen was wearing a simple navy skirt with an indigo blouse, fastened high at the neck. She had on lace-up shoes, but she could see that she was going to have to have boots if she was to be any help to John. The cabin was very small, and all of the families would sleep inside, because there were varmints out at night. And not just crawly ones or four-legged ones, she suspected. Mary had told her about the Comanches John and Luis and Isaac had been hunting when a calf was taken. She noted that a loaded shotgun was kept in a corner of the room, and she had no doubt that either of her companions could wield it if necessary. But she would ask John to teach her to shoot it, as well.

"You will have very pretty dresses from this material," Mary sighed as she touched the colored cottons of many prints and designs.

"*We* will have many pretty dresses," Ellen said, busily filling a bobbin for the sewing machine. She looked up at stunned expressions. "Surely you did not think I could use this much fabric by myself? There is enough here for all of us, I should imagine. And it will take less for the girls," she added, with a warm smile at them.

Mary actually turned away, and Ellen was horrified that she'd hurt the other woman's feelings. She jumped up from the makeshift chair John had cobbled together from tree limbs. "Mary, I'm sorry, I . . . !"

Mary turned back to her, tears running down her cheeks. "It's just, I haven't had a dress of my own, a new dress, in my whole life. Only hand-me-downs from my mistress, and they had to be torn up or used up first."

Ellen didn't know what to say. Her face was shocked.

Mary wiped away the tears. She looked at the other woman curiously. "You don't know about slaves, do you, Mrs. Ellen?"

"I know enough to be very sorry that some people think they can own other people," she replied carefully. "My family never did."

Mary forced a smile. "Mr. John brought us out here after the war. We been lucky. Two of our kids are lost forever, you know," she added matter-of-factly. "They got sold just before the war. And one of them got beat to death."

Ellen's eyes closed. She shuddered. It was overwhelming. Tears ran down her cheeks.

"Oh, now, Mrs., don't you . . . don't you do that!" Mary gathered her close and rocked her. "Don't you cry. Wherever my babies gone, they free now, don't you see. Alive or dead, they free."

The tears ran even harder.

"It was just as bad for Juana," Mary said through her own tears. "Two of her little boys got shot. This man got drunk and thought they was Indians. He just killed them right there in the road where they was playing, and he didn't even look back. He rode off laughing. Luis told the *federales*, but they couldn't find the man. That was years ago, before Mr. John's uncle hired Luis to work here, but Juana never forgot them little boys."

Ellen drew back and pulled a handkerchief out of her sleeve. She wiped Mary's eyes and smiled sadly. "We live in a bad world."

Mary smiled. "It's gonna get better," she said. "You wait and see."

"Better," Juana echoed, nodding, smiling. *"Mas bueno."*

"Mas . . . bueno?" Ellen repeated.

Juana chuckled. "*¡!Vaya! Muy bien!* Very good!"

Mary smiled. "You just spoke your first words of Spanish!"

"Perhaps you can teach me to speak Spanish," Ellen said to Juana.

"*Señora,* it will be my pleasure!" the woman answered, and smiled beautifully.

"I expect to learn a great deal, and very soon," Ellen replied.

That was an understatement. During her first week of residence, she became an integral part of John's extended family. She learned quite a few words of Spanish, including some range language that shocked John when she repeated it to him with a wicked grin.

"You stop that," he chastised. "Your father will have me shot if he hears you!"

She only chuckled, helping Mary put bread on the table. She was learning to make bread that didn't bounce, but it was early days yet. "My father thinks I will be begging him to come and get me within two weeks. He is in for a surprise!"

"I got the surprise," John had to admit, smiling at her. "You fit right in that first day." He looked from her to the other women, all wearing new dresses that they'd pieced on Ellen's sewing machine. He shook his head. "You three ought to open a dress shop in town."

Ellen glanced at Mary and Juana with pursed lips and twinkling eyes. "You know, that's not really such a bad idea, John," she said after a minute. "It would make us a little extra money. We could buy more barbed wire and we might even be able to afford a milk cow!"

John started to speak, but Mary and Juana jumped right in, and before he ate the first piece of bread, the women were already making plans.

CHAPTER FOUR

Ellen had John drive her into town the following Saturday, to the dry goods store. She spoke with Mr. Alton, the owner.

"I know there must be a market for inexpensive dresses in town, Mr. Alton," she said, bright-eyed. "You order them and keep them in stock, but the ones you buy are very expensive, and most ranch women can't afford them. Suppose I could supply you with simple cotton dresses, ready-made, at half the price of the ones you special order for customers?"

He lifted both eyebrows. "But, Mrs. Jacobs, your father is a wealthy man . . . !"

"My husband is not," she replied simply. "I must help him as I can." She smiled. "I have a knack for sewing, Mr. Alton, and I think I do quite good work. I also have two helpers who are learning how to use the machine. Would you let me try?"

He hesitated, adding up figures in his head. "All right," he said finally. "You bring me about six dresses, two each of small, medium and large ones, and we will see how they sell."

She grinned. "Done!" She went to the bolts of fabric he kept. "You must allow me credit, so that I can buy the material to make them with, and I will pay you back from my first orders."

He hesitated again. Then he laughed. She was very shrewd. But, he noticed that the dress she was wearing was quite well-made. His women customers had complained about the lack of variety and simplicity in his ready-made dresses, which were mostly for evening and not everyday.

"I will give you credit," he said after a minute. He shook his head as he went to cut the cloth she wanted. "You are a shrewd businesswoman, Mrs. Jacobs," he said. "I'll have to watch myself, or I may end up working for you!"

Which amused her no end.

John was dubious about his wife's enterprise, but Ellen knew what she was doing. Within three weeks, she and the women had earned enough money with their dressmaking to buy not one, but two Jersey milk cows with nursing calves. These John was careful to keep separate from his Hereford bull. But besides the milk, they made butter and buttermilk, which they took into town with their dresses and sold to the local restaurant.

"I told you it would work," Ellen said to John one afternoon when she'd walked out to the makeshift corral where he and the men were branding new calves.

He smiled down at her, wiping sweat from his face with the sleeve of his shirt. "You are a wonder," he murmured with pride. "We're almost finished here. Want to learn to ride?"

"Yes!" she exclaimed. But she looked down at her cotton dress with a sigh. "But not in this, I fear."

John's eyes twinkled. "Come with me."

He led her to the back of the cabin, where he pulled out a sack he'd hidden there. He offered it to her.

She opened it and looked inside. There was a man's cotton shirt, a pair of boots, and a pair of dungarees in it. She unfolded the dungarees and held them up to herself. "They'll just fit!" she exclaimed.

"I had Mr. Alton at the dry goods store measure one of your dresses for the size. He said they should fit even after shrinkage when you wash them."

"Oh, John, thank you!" she exclaimed. She stood on tiptoe and kissed him on the cheek.

He chuckled. "Get them on, then, and I'll teach you to mount a horse. I've got a nice old one that Luis brought with him. He's gentle."

"I won't be a minute!" she promised, darting back into the cabin.

John was at the corral when she came back out. She'd borrowed one of John's old hats and it covered most of her face as well as her bundled-up hair. She looked like a young boy in the rig, and he chuckled.

"Do I look ridiculous?" she worried.

"You look fine," he said diplomatically, his eyes twinkling. "Come along and meet Jorge."

He brought forward a gentle-looking old chestnut horse who lowered his head and nudged at her hand when she extended it. She stroked his forehead and smiled.

"Hello, old fellow," she said softly. "We're going to be great friends, aren't we?"

John pulled the horse around by its bridle and taught Ellen how to mount like a cowboy. Then, holding the reins, he led her around the yard, scattering their new flock of chickens along the way.

"They won't lay if we frighten them," Ellen worried.

He looked up at her with a grin. "How did you know that?"

"Mary taught me."

"She and Juana are teaching you a lot of new skills," he mused. "I liked the biscuits this morning, by the way."

Her heart skipped. "How did you know that I made them?"

"Because you watched every bite I took."

"Oh, dear."

He only laughed. "I am constantly amazed by you," he confessed as they turned away from the cabin and went toward the path that led through the brush to a large oak tree. "Honestly, I never thought you'd be able to live in such deprivation. Especially after . . . Ellen?"

He'd heard a faint scraping sound, followed by a thud. When he turned around, Ellen was sitting up in the dirt, looking stunned.

He threw the reins over the horse's head and ran to where she was sitting, his heart in his throat. "Ellen, are you hurt?!"

She glared up at him. "Did you not notice the tree limb, John?" she asked with a meaningful glance in its direction.

"Obviously not," he murmured sheepishly. "Did you?" he added.

She burst out laughing. “Only when it hit me.”

He chuckled as he reached down and lifted her up into his arms. It was the first time she’d been picked up in her adult life, and she gasped, locking her hands behind his neck so that she didn’t fall.

His green eyes met her blue ones at point blank range. The laughter vanished as suddenly as it had come. He studied her pert little nose, her high cheekbones, her pretty bow of a mouth. She was looking, too, her gaze faintly possessive as she noted the hard, strong lines of his face and the faint scars she found there. His eyes were very green at the proximity, and his mouth looked hard and firm. He had high cheekbones, too, and a broad forehead. His hair was thick under the wide-brimmed hat he wore, and black. His ears were, like his nose, of imposing size. The hands supporting her were big, too, like his booted feet.

“I have never been carried since I was a child,” she said in a hushed, fascinated tone.

“Well, I don’t usually make a practice of carrying women, either,” he confessed. His chiseled lips split in a smile. “You don’t weigh much.”

"I am far too busy becoming an entrepreneur to gain weight," she confessed.

"A what?"

She explained the word.

"You finished school, I reckon," he guessed.

She nodded. "I wanted to go to college, but Father does not think a woman should be overeducated."

"Bull," John said inelegantly. "My mother educated herself and even learned Latin, which she taught me. If we have daughters, they'll go to college."

She beamed, thinking of children. "I should like to have children."

He pursed his lips and lifted an eyebrow. His smile was sheer wickedness.

She laughed and buried her face in his throat, embarrassed. But he didn't draw back. His arms contracted around her and she felt his breath catch as he enveloped her soft breasts against the hard wall of his chest.

She felt unsettled. Her arms tightened around his strong neck and she shivered. She had never been held so close to a man's body. It was disconcerting. It was . . . delightful.

His cheek slid against hers so that he could find her soft lips with his mouth. He kissed her slowly, gently, with aching respect. When he pulled back, her lips followed. With a rough groan, he kissed her again. This time, there was less respect and more blatant hunger in the mouth that ravished hers.

She moaned softly, which brought him to his senses immediately. He drew back, his green eyes glittering with feeling. He wasn't breathing steadily anymore. Neither was she.

"We would have to climb a tree to find much privacy, and even then, the boys would probably be sitting in the branches," he said in a hunted tone.

She understood what he meant and flushed. But she laughed, too, because it was very obvious that he found her as attractive as she found him. She smiled into his eyes.

"One day, we will have a house as big as a barn, with doors that lock!" she assured him.

He chuckled softly. "Yes. But for now, we must be patient." He put her back on her feet with a long sigh. "Not that I feel patient," he added rakishly.

She laughed. "Nor I." She looked up at him demurely. "I suppose you have kissed a great many girls."

"Not so many," he replied. "And none as unique as you." His eyes were intent on her flushed face. "I made the best bargain of my life when I enticed you into marriage, Ellen Colby."

"Thank you," she said, stumbling over the words.

He pushed back a lock of disheveled dark hair that had escaped from under her hat. "It never occurred to me that a city woman, an aristocrat, would be able to survive living like this. I have felt guilty any number of times when I watched you carry water to the house, and wash clothes as the other women do. I know that you had maids to do such hard labor when you lived at home."

"I am young and very strong," she pointed out. "Besides, I have never found a man whom I respected enough to marry, until now. I believe you will make an empire here, in these wilds. But even if I didn't believe it, I would still be proud to take your name. You are unique, also."

His eyes narrowed. He bent again and kissed her eyelids shut, with breathless tenderness. "I will work hard to be worthy of your trust, Ellen. I will try never to disappoint you."

She smiled. "And you will promise never

to run me under oak limbs again?" she teased.

"You imp!" He laughed uproariously, hugging her to him like a big brother. "You scamp! What joy you bring to my days."

"And you to mine," she replied, hugging him back.

"Daddy! Mr. John and Mrs. Ellen are spooning right here in the middle of the road!" one of Isaac and Mary's boys yelled.

"Scatter, you varmints, I'm kissing my wife!" John called in mock-rage.

There was amused laughter and the sound of brush rustling.

"So much for the illusion of privacy," Ellen said, pulling back from him with a wistful sigh. "Shall we get back to the business at hand? Where's my horse?"

John spied him in the brush, munching on some small green growth of grass he had found there. "He's found something nice to eat, I'll wager," he said.

"I'll fetch him," Ellen laughed, and started into the brush.

"Ellen, stop!"

John's voice, full of authority and fear, halted her with one foot in the act of rising. She stopped and stood very still. He was cursing, using words Ellen had never heard in her life. "Isaac!" he tacked onto the end, "fetch my shotgun! Hurry!"

Ellen closed her eyes. She didn't have to look down to know why he was so upset. She could hear a rustling sound, like crackling leaves, like softly frying bacon. She had never seen a rattlesnake, but during her visit to Texas with her father, she had heard plenty about them from local people. Apparently they liked to lie in wait and strike out at unsuspecting people who came near them. They could cause death with a bite, or extreme pain and sickness. Ellen was mortally afraid of snakes, in any event. But John would save her. She knew he would.

There were running feet. Crashing brush. The sound of something being thrown and caught, and then the unmistakable sound of a hammer being pulled back.

"Stand very still, darling," John told her huskily. "Don't move . . . a muscle!"

She swallowed, her eyes still closed. She held her breath. There was a horrifying report, like the sound of thunder and lightning striking, near her feet. Flying dirt hit her dungarees. She heard furious thrashing and opened her eyes. For the first time, she looked down. A huge rattlesnake lay dismembered nearby, still writhing in the hot sun.

"Ellen, it didn't strike you?" John asked at once, wrapping her up in the arm that wasn't supporting the shotgun. "You're all right?"

"I am, thanks to you," she whispered, almost collapsing against him. "What a scare!"

"For both of us," he said curtly. He bent and kissed the breath out of her, still shaken from the experience. "Don't ever march into the brush without looking first!"

She smiled under his lips. "You could have caught the brush on fire with that language," she murmured reproachfully. "Indeed, I think the snake was shocked to death by it!"

He laughed, and kissed her harder. She kissed him back, only belatedly aware of running feet and exclamations when the snake was spotted.

He linked his big hand into her small one. "Luis, bring the horse, if you please. I think we've had enough riding practice for one day!"

"Si, señor," Luis agreed with a chuckle.

That evening around the campfire all the talk was of the close call Ellen had with the snake.

"You're on your way to being a living

legend," John told her as they roasted the victim of his shotgun over the darting orange and yellow tongues of flame. "Not to mention the provider of this delicious delicacy. Roasted rattler."

Ellen, game as ever, was soon nibbling on her own chunk of it. "It tastes surprisingly like chicken," she remarked.

John glowered at her. "It does not."

She grinned at him, and his heart soared. He grinned back.

"If you want another such treat, you will have to teach me how to shoot a gun," she proposed. "I am never walking into a rattler's mouth again, not even to provide you with supper!"

"Fair deal," he responded, while the others laughed uproariously.

In the days that followed, Ellen learned with hard work and sore muscles the rudiments of staying on a horse through the long days of watching over John's growing herd of cattle.

She also learned how not to shoot a shotgun. Her first acquaintance with the heavy double-barreled gun was a calamity. Having shouldered it too lightly, the report slammed the butt back into her shoulder and gave her a large, uncomfortable bruise.

They had to wait until it healed before she could try again. The one good thing was that it made churning butter almost impossible, and she grinned as she watched Mary shoulder that chore.

"You hurt your shoulder on purpose," Mary chided with laughing dark eyes. "So you wouldn't have to push this dasher up and down in the churn."

"You can always get Isaac to teach you how to shoot, and use the same excuse," Ellen pointed out.

Mary grinned. "Not me. I am not going near a shotgun, not even to get out of such chores!"

Juana agreed wholeheartedly. "Too much bang!"

"I'll amen that," Mary agreed.

"I like it," Ellen mused. She liked even more knowing that John was afraid for her, that he cared about her. He'd even called her "darling" when he'd shot the snake. He wasn't a man to use endearments normally, which made the verbal slip even more pleasurable. She'd been walking around in a fog of pleasure ever since the rattler almost bit her. She was in love. She hoped that he was feeling something similar, but he'd been much too busy with work to hang around her, except at night.

And then there was a very large audience. She sighed, thinking that privacy must be the most valuable commodity on earth. Although she was growing every day fonder of her companions, she often wished them a hundred miles away, so that she had even an hour alone with her husband. But patience was golden, she reminded herself. She must wait and hope for that to happen. Right now, survival itself was a struggle.

So was the shotgun. Her shoulder was well enough for a second try a week later. Two new complications, unbeknownst to Ellen, had just presented themselves. There were new mud puddles in the front yard, and her father had come to town and rented a buggy to ride out to visit his only child.

Ellen aimed the shotgun at a tree. The resulting kick made the barrel fly up. A wild turkey, which had been sitting on a limb, suddenly fell to the ground in a limp heap. And Ellen went backward right into the deepest mud puddle the saturated yard could boast.

At that particular moment, her father pulled up in front of the cabin.

Her father looked from Ellen to the turkey to the mud puddle to John. "I see that you are teaching my daughter to bathe and hunt at the same time," he remarked.

Ellen scrambled to her feet, wiping her hair back with a muddy hand. She was so disheveled, and so dirty, that it was hard for her immaculate father to find her face at all.

He grimaced. "Ellen, darling, I think it might not be a bad idea if you came home with me," he began uneasily.

She tossed her head, slinging mud onto John, who was standing next to her looking concerned. "I'm only just learning to shoot, Father," she remarked proudly. "No one is proficient at first. Isn't that so, John?"

"Uh, yes," John replied, but without his usual confidence.

Her father looked from one to the other and then to the turkey. "I suppose buying meat from the market in town is too expensive?" he asked.

"I like variety. We had rattlesnake last week, in fact," Ellen informed him. "It was delicious."

Her father shook his head. "Your grandmother is going to have heart failure if I tell her what I've seen here. And young man, this house of yours . . . !" He spread an expansive hand helplessly.

“The sooner we get *our* spur line,” Ellen told her father, “the quicker we will have a real house instead of merely a cabin.”

John nodded hopefully.

Terrance Colby sighed heavily. “I’ll see what I can do,” he promised.

They both smiled. “Will you stay for dinner?” Ellen invited, glancing behind her. She grinned. “We’re having turkey!”

Her father declined, unwilling to share the sad surroundings that his daughter seemed to find so exciting. There were three families living in that one cabin, he noted, and he wasn’t certain that he was democratic enough to appreciate such close quarters. It didn’t take a mind reader to note that Ellen and John had no privacy. That might be an advantage, he mused, if Ellen decided to come home. There would be no complications. But she seemed happy as a lark, and unless he was badly mistaken, that young man John Jacobs was delighted with her company. His wife’s mother was not going to be happy when he got up enough nerve to tell her what had happened to Ellen. She was just on her way home from a vacation in Italy. Perhaps the ship would be blown off course and she would not get home for several months, he mused. Otherwise, Ellen was going to have a very unhappy visitor in the near future.

He did make time to see John's growing herd of cattle, and he noticed that the young man had a fine lot of very healthy steers. He'd already seen how enterprising Ellen was with her dressmaking and dairy sales. Now he saw a way to help John become quickly self-sufficient.

Word came the following week that Ellen's father was busy buying up right of way for the spur that would run to John's ranch. Not only that, he had become a customer for John's yearling steers, which he planned to feed to the laborers who were already hard at work on another stretch of his railroad. The only difficulty was that John was going to have to drive the steers north to San Antonio for Terrance Colby. Colby would be there waiting for him in a week. That wasn't a long cattle drive, certainly not as far as Kansas, but south Texas was still untamed and dangerous country. It would be risky. But John knew it would be worth the risk if he could deliver the beef.

So John and his men left, reluctantly on John's part, to drive the steers north. He and his fellow cowhands went around to all the other ranches, gathering up their steers, making sure they appropriated only the cattle that bore their 3J brand for the drive.

"I don't want to go," John told Ellen as they stood together, briefly alone, at the corral. "But I must protect our investment. There will be six of us to drive the herd, and we are all armed and well able to handle any trouble. Isaac and the older boys are going with me, but Luis will stay here to look after the livestock and all of you."

She sighed, smoothing her arms over the sleeves of his shirt, enjoying the feel of the smooth muscles under it. "I do not like the idea of you going away. But I know that it is necessary, so I'll be brave."

"I don't like leaving you, either," he said bluntly. He bent and kissed her hungrily. "When I return, perhaps we can afford a single night away from here," he whispered roughly. "I am going mad to have you in my arms without a potential audience!"

"As I am," she choked, kissing him back hungrily.

He lifted her clear of the ground in his embrace, flying as they kissed without restraint. Finally, he forced himself to put her back down and he stepped away. There was a ruddy flush on his high cheekbones, and his green eyes were fierce. Her face was equally flushed, but her eyes were soft and dreamy, and her mouth was swollen.

She smiled up at him bravely, despite her concern. "Don't get shot."

He grimaced. "I'll do my best. You stay within sight of the cabin and Luis, even when you're milking those infernal cows. And don't go to town without him."

She didn't mention that it would be suicide to take Luis away from guarding the cattle, even for that long. She and the women would have to work something out, so that they could sell their dresses and butter and milk in town. But she would spare him the worry.

"We'll be very careful," she promised.

He sighed, his hand resting on the worn butt of his .45 caliber pistol. "We'll be back as soon as humanly possible. Your father . . ."

"If he comes to town, I'll go there to wait for you," she promised, a lie, because she'd never leave Mary and Juana by themselves, even with Luis and a shotgun around.

"Possibly that's what you should do, anyway," he murmured thoughtfully.

"I can't leave here now," she replied. "There's too much at stake. I'll help take care of our ranch. You take care of our profit margin."

He chuckled, surprised out of his worries. "I'll be back before you miss me too much," he said, bending to kiss her again, briefly. "Stay close to the cabin."

"I will. Have a safe trip."

He swung into the saddle, shouting for Isaac and the boys. The women watched them ride away. The cattle had already been pooled in a nearby valley, and the drovers were ready to get underway. As Ellen watched her tall husband ride away, she realized why he'd wanted his railroad spur so badly. Not only was it dangerous to drive cattle a long way to a railhead, but the potential risk to the men and animals was great. Not only was there a constant threat from thieves, there were floods and thunderstorms that could decimate herds. She prayed that John and Isaac and the men going with them would be safe. It was just as well that Luis was staying at the ranch to help safeguard the breeding bulls and cows, and the calves that were too young for market. Not that she was going to shirk her own responsibilities, Ellen thought stubbornly. Nobody was stealing anything around here while she could get her hands on a gun!

* * *

The threat came unexpectedly just two days after John and the others had left south Texas for San Antonio on the cattle drive.

Ellen had just carried a bucketful of milk to the kitchen when she peered out the open, glassless window at two figures on horseback, watching the cabin. She called softly to Juana and Mary.

Juana crossed herself. "It is Comanches!" she exclaimed. "They come to raid the cattle!"

"Well, they're not raiding them today," Ellen said angrily. "I'll have to ride out and get Luis and the boys," she said. "There's nothing else for it, and I'll have to go bareback. I'll never have time to saddle a horse with them sitting out there."

"It is too dangerous," Juana exclaimed. "You can hardly ride a saddled horse, and those men are Comanches. They are the finest riders of any men, even my Luis. You will never outrun them!"

Ellen muttered under her breath. They had so few cattle that even the loss of one or two could mean the difference between bankruptcy and survival. Well, she decided, there was only one thing to do. She grabbed up the shotgun, loaded it, and started out the back door, still in her dress and apron.

"No!" Mary almost screamed. "Are you crazy? Do you know what they do to white women?!"

Ellen didn't say a word. She kept walking, her steps firm and sure.

She heard frantic calls behind her, but she didn't listen. She and John had a ranch. These were her cattle as much as his. She wasn't about to let any thieves come and carry off her precious livestock!

The two Comanches saw her coming and gaped. They didn't speak. They sat on their horses with their eyes fixed, wide, at the young woman lugging a shotgun toward them.

One of them said something to the other one, who laughed and nodded.

She stopped right in front of them, lifted the shotgun, sighted along it and cocked it.

"This is my ranch," she said in a firm, stubborn tone. "You aren't stealing my cattle!"

There was pure admiration in their eyes. They didn't reach for the rifles lying across their buckskinned laps. They didn't try to ride her down. They simply watched her.

The younger of the two Indians had long

pigtails and a lean, handsome face. His eyes, she noted curiously, were light.

"We have not come to steal cattle," the young one said in passable English. "We have come to ask Big John for work."

"Work?" she stammered.

He nodded. "We felt guilty that we butchered one of his calves. We had come far and were very hungry. We will work to pay for the calf. We hear from the Mexican people that he is also fair," he added surprisingly. "We know that he looks only at a man's work. He does not consider himself better than men of other colors. This is very strange. We do not understand it. Your people have just fought a terrible war because you wanted to own other people who had dark skin. Yet Big John lives with these people. Even with the Mexicans. He treats them as family."

"Yes," she said. She slowly uncocked the shotgun and lowered it to her side. "That is true."

The younger one smiled at her. "We know more about horses than even his vaquero, who knows much," he said without conceit. "We will work hard. When we pay back the cost of the calf, he can pay us what he thinks is fair."

She chuckled. "It's not really a big cabin,

and it has three families living in it," she began.

They laughed. "We can make a teepee," the older one said, his English only a little less accented than the younger one's.

"I say," she exclaimed, "can you teach me to shoot a bow?!"

The younger one threw back his head and laughed uproariously. "Even his woman is brave," he told the older one. "Now do you believe me? This man is not as others with white skin."

"I believe you."

"Come along, then," Ellen said, turning. "I'll introduce you to . . . Luis! Put that gun down!" she exclaimed angrily when she saw the smaller man coming toward them with two pistols leveled. "These are our two new horse wranglers," she began. She stopped. "What are your names?" she asked.

"I am called Thunder," the young one said. "He is Red Wing."

"I am Ellen Jacobs," she said, "and that is Luis. Say hello, Luis."

The Mexican lowered his pistols and reholstered them with a blank stare at Ellen.

"Say hello," she repeated.

"Hello," he obliged, and he nodded.

The Comanches nodded back. They rode up to the cabin and dismounted. The women in the cabin peered out nervously.

"Luis will show you where to put your horses," Ellen told them. "We have a lean-to. Someday, we will have a barn!"

"Need bigger teepee first," Red Wing murmured, eyeing the cabin. "Bad place to live. Can't move house when floor get dirty."

"Yes, well, it's warm," Ellen said helplessly.

The young Comanche, Thunder, turned to look at her. "You are brave," he said with narrow light eyes. "Like my woman."

"She doesn't live with you?" she asked hesitantly.

He smiled gently. "She is stubborn, and wants to live in a cabin far away," he replied. "But I will bring her back here one day." He nodded and followed after Luis with his friend.

Juana and Mary came out of the cabin with worried expressions. "You going to let Indians live with us?" Juana exclaimed. "They kill us all!"

"No, they won't," Ellen assured them. "You'll see. They're going to be an asset!"

CHAPTER FIVE

The Comanches did know more about horses than even Luis did, and they were handy around the place. They hunted game, taught Luis how to tan hides, and set about building a teepee out behind the cabin.

"Very nice," Ellen remarked when it was finished. "It's much roomier than the cabin."

"Easy to keep clean," Red Wing agreed. "Floor get dirty, move teepee."

She laughed. He smiled, going off to help Thunder with a new corral Juan was building.

John rode back in with Isaac and stopped short at the sight of a towering teepee next to the cabin he'd left two weeks earlier.

His hand went to his pistol as he thought of terrible possibilities that would explain its presence.

But Ellen came running out of the cabin, followed by Mary and Juana, laughing and waving.

John kicked his foot out of the stirrup of his new saddle and held his arm down to welcome Ellen as she leaped up into his arms. He kissed her hungrily, feeling as if he'd come home for the first time in his life.

He didn't realize how long that kiss lasted until he felt eyes all around him. He lifted his head to find two tall Comanches standing shoulder to shoulder with Juan and the younger boys and girls of the group, along with Juana and Mary.

"Bad habit," Thunder remarked disapprovingly.

"Bound to upset horse," Red Wing agreed, nodding.

"What the hell . . . !" John exclaimed.

"They're our new horse wranglers," Ellen said quickly. "That's Thunder, and that's Red Wing."

"They taught us how to make parfleche bags," Juana's eldest daughter exclaimed, showing one with beautiful beadwork.

"And how to make bows and arrows!" the next youngest of Isaac's sons seconded, showing his.

"And quivers," Luis said, resigned to being fired for what John would surely consider bad judgment in letting two Comanches near the women. He stood with his sombrero against his chest. "You may fire me if you wish."

"If you fire me, I'm going with them," Isaac's second son replied, pointing toward the Indians.

John shook his head, laughing uproariously. "I expect there'll be a lynch mob out here any day now," he sighed.

Everybody grinned.

Ellen beamed up at him. "Well, they certainly do know how to train horses, John," she said.

"Your woman meet us with loaded shotgun," Red Wing informed him. "She has strong spirit."

"And great heart," Thunder added. "She says we can work for you. We stay?"

John sighed. "By all means. All we need now is an Eskimo," he murmured to Ellen under his breath.

She looped her arms around his neck and kissed him. "Babies would be nice," she whispered.

He went scarlet, and everyone laughed.

"I got enough for the steers to buy a new bull," John told her. "Saddles for the horses we have, and four new horses," he added. "They're coming in with the rest of the drovers. I rode ahead to make sure you were all right."

She cuddled close to him as they stood out behind the cabin in a rare moment alone. "We had no trouble at all. Well, except for the Comanches, but they turned out to be friends anyway."

"You could have blown me over when I saw that teepee," he confessed. "We've had some hard battles with Comanches in the past, over stolen livestock. And I know for a fact that two Comanches ate one of my calves . . ."

"They explained that," she told him contentedly. "They were hungry, but they didn't want to steal. They came here to work out the cost of the calf, and then to stay on, if you'll keep them. I think they decided that it's better to join a strong foe than oppose him. That was the reason they gave me, at least."

"Well, I must admit, these two Comanches are unusual."

"The younger one has light eyes."

"I noticed." He didn't add what he was certain of — that these two Comanches were the fugitives that the deputy marshal in Sutherland Springs had been looking for. Fortunately for them, James Graham had headed up beyond San Antonio to pursue them, acting on what now seemed to be a very bad tip.

She lifted her head and looked up at him.

"They rode up and just sat there. I loaded my shotgun and went out to see what they wanted."

"You could have been killed," he pointed out.

"It's what you would have done, in my place," she reminded him, smiling gently. "I'm not afraid of much. And I've learned from you that appearances can be deceptive."

"You take chances."

"So do you."

He sighed. "You're learning bad habits from me."

She smiled and snuggled close. "Red Wing is going to make us a teepee of our own very soon." She kissed him, and was kissed back hungrily.

"Yesterday not be soon enough for that teepee," came a droll accented voice from nearby.

Red Wing was on the receiving end of two pairs of glaring eyes. He shrugged and walked off noiselessly, chuckling to himself.

John laughed. "Amen," he murmured.

"John, there's just one other little thing," Ellen murmured as she stood close to him.

"What now? You hired a gunslinger to feed the chickens?"

"I don't know any gunslingers. Be serious."

"All right. What?"

"My grandmother sent me a telegram. She's coming out here to save me from a life of misery and poverty."

He lifted his head. "Really!"

She drew in a soft breath. "I suppose she'll faint dead away when she sees this place, but I'm not going to be dragged back East by her or an army. I belong here."

"Yes, you do," John replied. "Although you certainly deserve better than this, Ellen," he said softly. He touched her disheveled hair. "I promise you, it's only going to get better."

She smiled. "I know that. We're going to have an empire, all our own."

"You bet we are."

"Built with our own two hands," she murmured, reaching up to kiss him, "and the help of our friends. All we need is each other."

"Need teepee worse," came Red Wing's voice again.

"Listen here," John began.

"Your horse got colic," the elder of the

Comanches stood his ground. "What you feed him?"

"He ate corn," John said belligerently. "I gave him a feed bucket full!"

The older man scoffed. "No wonder he got colic. I fix."

"Corn is good for horses, and I know what to do for colic!"

"Sure. Not feed horse corn. Feed him grass. We build teepee tomorrow."

John still had his mouth open when the older man stalked off again.

"Indian ponies only eat grass," Ellen informed him brightly. "They think grain is bad for horses."

"You've learned a lot," he remarked.

"More than you might realize," she said dryly. She reached up to John's ear. "These two Comanches are running from the army. But I don't think they did anything bad, and I told Mr. Alton that I saw two Comanches heading north at a dead run. He told the . . ."

". . . deputy marshal," he finished for her, exasperated.

"When you get to know them, you'll think they're good people, too," she assured him. "Besides, they're teaching me things I can't learn anywhere else. I can track a deer," she counted off her new skills, "weave a mat, make a bed out of pine straw, do beadwork, shoot a bow and arrow, and tan a hide."

"Good Lord, woman!" he exclaimed, impressed.

She grinned. "And I'm going to learn to hunt just as soon as you take me out with my shotgun."

He sighed. This was going to become difficult if any of her people stopped by to check on her. He didn't want to alienate them, but this couldn't continue.

"Ellen, what do you think about schooling?" he asked gently.

She blinked. "Excuse me?"

"Well, do any of the children know how to read and write?"

She hadn't considered that. "I haven't asked, but I don't expect they can. It was not legal for slaves to be taught such things, and I know that Juana can't even read Spanish, although it is her native tongue."

"The world we build will need educated people," he said thoughtfully. "It must start with the children, with this new generation. Don't you agree?"

"Yes," she said, warming quickly to the idea. "Educated people will no longer have to work at menial jobs, where they are at the mercy of others."

"That is exactly what I think. So, why don't you start giving the children a little book learning, in the evenings, after supper?" he suggested.

She smiled brightly. "You know, that's a very good idea. But, I have no experience as a teacher."

"All you will need are some elementary books and determination," he said. "I believe there is a retired schoolteacher in Victoria, living near the blacksmith. Shall I take you to see him?"

She beamed. "Would you?"

"Indeed I would. We'll go up there tomorrow," he replied, watching her consider the idea. If nothing else, it would spare her the astonished surprise of her people if they ever came to visit and found Ellen in dungarees and muddy boots skinning out a deer.

He drove her to Victoria the next morning in the small, dilapidated buggy he'd managed to afford from his cattle sales, hitched to one of the good horses he'd also acquired. Fortunately it took to pulling a buggy right away. Some horses didn't, and people died in accidents when they panicked and ran away.

The schoolteacher was long retired, but

he taught Ellen the fundamentals she would need to educate small children. He also had a basic reader, a grammar book and a spelling book, which he gave to Ellen with his blessing. She clutched them like priceless treasure all the way back down the dusty road to the 3J Ranch.

"Do you think the Brown and the Rodriguez families will let me teach the children?" she wondered, a little worried after the fact. "They might not believe in education."

"Luis and Isaac can't even sign a paper," he told her. "They have to make an 'x' on a piece of paper and have me witness it. If they ever leave the ranch, they need to know how to read and write so that nobody will take advantage of them."

She looked at him with even more admiration than usual. He was very handsome to her, very capable and strong. She counted her blessings every single day that he'd thought her marriageable.

"You really care for them, don't you?" she asked softly.

"When the Union Army came through Atlanta, they burned everything in sight," he recalled, his face hardening. "Not just the big plantations where slaves were kept. They burned poor white people's houses, because they thought we all had slaves down south." He laughed coldly. "Sharecroppers don't own anything. Even the house we lived in belonged to the plantation owner. They set it ablaze and my sister and mother were trapped inside. They burned to death while my other sister and I stood outside and watched." He touched his lean cheek, where the old scars were still noticeable. "I tried to kill the cavalry officer responsible, but his men saved him. They gave me these," he touched his cheek. "I never kept slaves. I hid Isaac and Mary in the root cellar when they ran away from the overseer. I couldn't save their oldest son, but Mary was pregnant. She and Isaac saved me from the Union Army," he said with a sigh. "They pleaded for my life. Shocked the cavalry into sparing me and my oldest sister. Isaac helped me bury my mother and my younger sister." He looked down at her soft, compassionate expression. "My sister went to North Carolina to live with a cousin, but I wanted to go to my uncle in Texas. Isaac and Mary had no place else to go, so they traveled with me. They said they wanted to start over, but they didn't fool me. They came with me to save me from the Union Army if I got in trouble.

Those two never forget a debt. I owe them everything. My life. That's why they're partners with me."

"And how did you meet Luis and Juana?" she asked.

"Luis was the only cowboy my uncle had who wasn't robbing him blind. Luis told me what the others had done, and I fired the lot. I took care of my uncle, with their help, and rounded up stray calves to start my herd." He chuckled. "The cabin was the only structure on the place. It got real crowded when Isaac and Mary moved in with me. Juana and Luis were going to live in the brush, but I insisted that we could all manage. We have. But it hasn't been easy."

"And now the Comanches are building teepees for us," she told him. "They've been hunting constantly to get enough skins. We're going to have privacy for the very first time. I mean . . ." She flushed at her own forwardness.

He reached for her small hand and held it tight. His eyes burned into hers. "I want nothing more in the world than to be alone with you, Camellia Ellen Jacobs," he said huskily. "The finest thing I ever did in my life was have the good sense to marry you!"

"Do you really think so?" she asked happily. "I am no beauty . . ."

"You have a heart as big as all outdoors and the courage of a wolf. I wouldn't trade you for a debutante."

She beamed, leaning against his broad shoulder. "And I would not trade you for the grandest gentleman who ever lived. Although I expect you will make a fine gentleman, when we have made our fortune."

He kissed her forehead tenderly. "You are my fortune," he said huskily.

"You mean, because my father is giving us a railroad spur for a wedding present," she said, confused.

He shook his head. "Because you are my most prized treasure," he whispered, and bent to kiss her mouth tenderly.

She kissed him back, shyly. "I had never kissed anyone until you came along," she whispered.

He chuckled. "You improve with practice!"

"John!" she chided.

He only laughed, letting her go to pay attention to the road. "We must get on down the road. It looks like rain." He gave her a roguish glance. "We would not want you to tumble into a mud puddle, Mrs. Jacobs."

"Are you ever going to forget that?" she moaned.

"In twenty years or so, perhaps," he said. "But I cannot promise. That is one of my most delightful memories. You were so game, and Sir Sydney was such a boor!"

"Indeed he was. I hope he marries for money and discovers that she has none."

"Evil girl," he teased.

She laughed. "Well, you will never be able to accuse ME of marrying you for your money," she said contentedly. "In twenty years or so," she added, repeating his own phrase, "you will be exceedingly rich. I just know it."

"I hope to break even, at least, and be able to pay my debts," he said. "But I would love to have a ranch as big as a state, Ellen, and the money to breed fine cattle, and even fine horses." He glanced at her. "Now that we have two extra horse wranglers, we can start building up our herd."

She only smiled. She was glad that she'd stood up to the Comanches. She wondered if they'd ever have wanted to work for them if she'd run away and hid.

The teepee the Comanches built for the couple was remarkably warm and clean. No sooner was it up than Ellen built a small cooking fire near its center and put on a black iron pot of stew to cook. Red Wing had already taught her how to turn the pole in the center to work the flap for letting smoke out while she cooked. She also learned that she was born to be a rancher's wife. Every chore came easily to her. She wasn't afraid of hard work, and she fell more in love with her roguish, unconventional husband every day. She did still worry about her grandmother coming down to rescue her. She had no intention of being carted off back East, where she would have to dress and act with decorum.

She sat the children down in the cabin one evening after she and the other women and older girls had cleared away the precious iron cookware and swished the tin plates and few utensils in a basin of soapy water and wiped them with a dishrag.

"What are we going to do?" one of Juana's daughters asked.

Ellen produced the books that the retired Victoria schoolteacher had given her, handling them like treasure.

"I'm going to teach you children to read and write," she told them.

Mary and Juana stood quietly by, so still that Ellen was made uneasy.

"Is it all right?" she asked the adults,

concerned, because she'd worried that they might think education superfluous.

"Nobody ever taught me to write my name," Mary said. "Nor Isaac, either. We can only make an x. Could you teach me to write? And read?"

"Me, too!" Juana exclaimed.

Their husbands looked as if they might bite their tongues off trying not to ask if they could learn, too, but they managed.

"You can all gather around and we'll let the older folk help show the young ones how to do it," she said, managing a way to spare the pride of the men in the process of teaching them as well.

"Yes, we can show them, *señora*," Luis said brightly.

"Sure we can," Isaac added with a big grin.

"Gather around, then." She opened the book with a huge smile and began the first lesson.

She looked down at the dungarees she was wearing with boots that John had bought her. She had on one of his big checked long-sleeved shirts, with the sleeves rolled up, and her hair was caught in a ponytail down her back. She checked the stew in her black cooking pot and wiped sweat from her brow with a weary hand. The Comanches had gathered pine straw from under the short-leafed pines in the thicket to make beds, which Ellen covered with quilts she and the other women had made in their precious free time. It wasn't a mansion, but she and John would have privacy for the first time that night. She thought of the prospect with joy and a certain amount of trepidation. Like most young women of her generation, her upbringing had been very strict and moral. She knew almost nothing of what happened between married people in the dark. What she didn't know made her nervous.

The sudden noise outside penetrated her thoughts. She heard voices, one raised and strident, and she ran out of the teepee and to the cabin to discover a well-dressed, elderly woman with two young men in immaculate suits exchanging heated words with Juana, who couldn't follow a thing they were saying. Mary was out with the others collecting more wood for the fireplace in the small cabin.

"Do you understand me?" the old woman was shouting. "I am looking for Ellen Colby!"

"Grandmother!" Ellen exclaimed when she recognized the woman.

Her grandmother Amelia Greene was standing beside the buggy beside two tall young men whom Ellen recognized as her cousins.

Amelia turned stiffly, her whole expression one of utter disapproval when she saw the way her granddaughter was dressed.

"Camellia Ellen Colby!" she exclaimed. "What has become of you!"

"Now, Grandmother," Ellen said gently, "you can't expect a pioneer wife to dress and act as a lady in a drawing room."

The older woman was not convinced. She was bristling with indignation. "You will get your things together and come home with me right away!" she demanded. "I am not leaving you here in the dirt with these peasants!"

Ellen's demeanor changed at once from one of welcome and uneasiness to one of pure outrage. She stuck both hands on her slender hips and glared at her grandmother.

"How dare you call my friends peasants!" she exclaimed furiously. She went to stand beside Juana. "Juana's husband Luis, and Mary's husband Isaac, are our partners in this ranching enterprise. They are no one's servants!"

Mary came to stand beside her as well,

and the children gathered around them. While the old woman and her companions were getting over that shock, John came striding up, with his gun-belt on, accompanied by Luis and Isaac and the two Comanche men.

Amelia Greene screeched loudly and jumped behind the tallest of her grandchildren.

"How much you want for old woman?" Red Wing asked deliberately, pointing at Amelia.

Amelia looked near to fainting.

Ellen laughed helplessly. "He's not serious," she assured her grandmother.

"I should hope not!" the tallest of her cousins muttered, glaring at him. "The very idea! Why do you allow Indians here?"

"These are our horse wranglers," Ellen said pointedly. "Red Wing and Thunder. And those are our partners, Luis Rodriguez and Isaac Brown. Gentlemen, my grandmother, Amelia Greene of New York City."

Nobody spoke.

John came forward to slide his arm around Ellen's waist. He was furious at the way her relatives were treating the people nearby.

"Hospitality is almost a religion to us out here in Texas," John drawled, although his green eyes were flashing like green diamonds. "But as you may notice, we have no facilities to accommodate visitors yet."

"You cannot expect that we would want to stay?" the shorter cousin asked indignantly. "Come, Grandmother, let us go back to town. Ellen is lost to us. Surely you can see that?"

Ellen glared at him. "Five years from now, cousin, you will not recognize this place. A lot of hard work is going to turn it into a showplace. . . ."

"Of mongrels!" her grandmother said haughtily.

"I'm sorry you feel that way, but I find your company equally taxing," Ellen shot back. "Now will you all please leave? I have chores, as do the others. Unlike you, I do not sit in the parlor waiting for other people to fetch and carry at my instructions."

The old woman glowered. "Very well, then, live out here in the wilds with savages! I only came to try and save you from a life of drudgery!"

"Pickles and bread," Ellen retorted haughtily. "You came hoping to entice me back into household slavery. Until I escaped you and came west with my father, I was your unpaid maidservant for most of my life."

"What else are you fit for?" her grandmother demanded. "You have no looks, no talent, no . . . !"

"She is lovely," John interrupted. "Gentle and kind and brave. She is no one's servant here, and she has freedom of a sort you will never know."

The old woman's eyes were poisonously intent. "She will die of hard work here, for certain!"

"On her own land, making her own empire," John replied tersely. "The road is that way," he added, pointing.

She tossed her head and sashayed back to the buggy, to be helped in by her grandsons, one of whom gave Ellen a wicked grin before he climbed in and took the reins.

"Drive on," Amelia said curtly. "We have no kinfolk here!"

"Truer words were never spoken," Ellen said sweetly. "Do have a safe trip back to town. Except for cattle thieves from Mexico and the bordering counties of Texas, and bank robbers, there should be nothing dangerous in your path. But I would drive very fast, if I were you!"

There were muttered, excited exchanges of conversation in the buggy before the tallest grandson used the buggy whip and the small vehicle raced forward down the dusty dirt road in the general direction of town.

"You wicked girl!" John exclaimed on a burst of laughter, hugging her close.

"So much for my rescuers," she murmured contentedly, hugging him back. "Now we can get back to work!"

That night, Ellen and John spent their first night alone, without prying eyes or ears, in the teepee the Comanches had provided for them.

"I am a little nervous," she confessed when John had put out the small fire and they were together in the darkness.

"That will not last," he promised, drawing her close. "We are both young, and we have all the years ahead to become more accustomed to each other. All you must remember is that I care more for you than for any woman I have ever known. You are my most prized treasure. I love you. I will spend my life trying to make you happy."

"John!" She pressed close to him and raised her face. "I will do the same. I adore you!"

He bent and kissed her softly, and then not so softly. Tender caresses gave way to stormy, devouring kisses. They sank to the makeshift mattress and there, locked tight in each others' arms, they gave way to the smoldering passion that had grown between them for long weeks. At first she was inhibited, but he was skillful and slow and tender. Very soon, her passion rose to meet his. The sharpness of passion was new between them, and as it grew, they became playful together. They laughed, and then the laughing stopped as they tasted the first sweet sting of mutual delight in the soft, enveloping darkness.

When Ellen finally fell asleep in John's arms, she thought that there had never been a happier bride in the history of Texas.

CHAPTER SIX

Ellen's grandmother and cousins went back East. Her father came regularly to visit them in their teepee, finding it touching and amusing at once that they were happy with so little. He even offered to loan them enough to build a bigger cabin, but they refused politely. All they wanted, Ellen reminded him, was a spur of the railroad.

That, too, was finally finished. John loaded his beef cattle into the cattle cars bound for the stockyards of the Midwest. The residents of the ranch settled into hard work and camaraderie, and all their efforts eventually resulted in increasing prosperity.

The first thing they did with their newfound funds was to add to the cattle herd. The second was to build individual cabins for the Rodriguez and Brown clans, replacing the teepees the Comanches had built for them. The Comanches, offered a handsome log cabin of their own, declined abruptly, although politely. They could never understand the white man's interest in a stationary house that had to be cleaned constantly, when it was so much easier to move the teepee to a clean spot! However, John and Ellen continued to live in their own teepee for the time being, as well, to save money.

A barn was the next project. As in all young communities, a barbecue and a quilting bee were arranged along with a barnraising. All the strong young men of the area turned out and the resulting barn and corral were quick fruit of their efforts. Other ranches were springing up around the 3J Ranch, although not as large and certainly not with the number of cattle and horses that John's now boasted.

The railroad spur, when it came, brought instant prosperity to the area it served. It grew and prospered even as some smaller towns in the area became ghost towns. Local citizens decided that they needed a name for their small town, which had actually grown up around the ranch itself even before the railroad came. They decided to call it Jacobsville, for John Jacobs, despite his protests. His hard work and lack of prejudice had made him good friends and dangerous enemies in the surrounding area. But when cattle were rustled and houses robbed, his was never among them. Bandits from over the border made a wide route around the ranch.

As the cattle herd grew and its refinement continued, the demand for Jacobs's beef grew as well. John bought other properties to go along with his own, along with barbed wire to fence in his ranges. He hired on new men as well, black drovers as well as Mexican and white. There was even a Chinese drover who had heard of the Jacobs ranch far away in Arizona and had come to it looking for a job. Each new addition to the ranch workforce was placed under the orders of either Luis or Isaac, and the number of outbuildings and line camps grew steadily.

Ellen worked right alongside the other women, adding new women to her dressmaking enterprise, until she had enough workers and enough stock to open a dress shop in their new town of Jacobsville. Mary and Juana took turns as proprietors while Ellen confined herself to sewing chair and sofa covers for the furniture in the new white clapboard house John had built her. She and her handsome husband grew closer by the day, but one thing was still missing from her happiness. Their marriage was entering into its second year with no hope of a child.

John never spoke of it, but Ellen knew he wanted children. So did she. It was a curious thing that their passion for each other was ever growing, but bore no fruit. Still, they had a good marriage and Ellen was happier than she ever dreamed of being.

In the second year of their marriage, his sister Jeanette came west on the train with her husband and four children to visit. Only then did Ellen learn the extent of the tragedy that had sent John west in the first place. The attack by the Union troops had mistakenly been aimed at the sharecroppers' cabin John and his mother and sisters occupied, instead of the house where the owner's vicious overseer lived. The house had caught fire and John's mother and elder sister had burned to death. John had not been able to save them. The attack had been meant for the overseer who had beaten Isaac and Mary's son to death, along with many other slaves. John was told, afterward, but his grief was so sweeping that he hardly understood what was said to him. His sister made sure that he did know. The cavalry officer had apologized to her, and given her money for the trip to North Carolina, unbeknownst to John. His sister obviously adored him, and he was a doting uncle to her children.

She understood John's dark moods better after that, the times when he wanted to be alone, when he went hunting and never brought any wild game home with him. Ellen and Jeanette became close almost at once, and wrote to each other regularly even when Jeanette and her family went home to North Carolina.

Deputy Marshal James Graham had come by unexpectedly and mentioned to John that he hadn't been able to find the two Comanche fugitives who were supposed to have shot a white man over a horse. It turned out that the white man had cheated the Comanches and had later been accused of cheating several army officers in horse trading deals. He was arrested, tried and sent to prison. So, Graham told John, the Comanches weren't in trouble anymore. Just in case John ever came across them.

Thunder and Red Wing, told of the white man's arrest, worked a few months longer for John and then headed north with their wages. Ellen was sad to see them go, but Thunder had promised that they would meet again one day.

The Maxwells came to visit often from Scotland, staying in the beautiful white

Victorian house John later built for his beloved wife. They gave the couple the benefit of their extensive experience of horses, and John branched out into raising thoroughbreds. Eventually a thoroughbred of the lineage from his ranch would win the Triple Crown.

Years passed with each year bringing new prosperity to the 3J Ranch. One May morning, Ellen unexpectedly fainted at a church social. John carried her to the office of their new doctor, who had moved in just down the boardwalk from the new restaurant and hotel.

The doctor examined her and, when John had been invited into the examination room, grinned at him. "You are to be a father, young man," he said. "Congratulations!"

John looked at Ellen as if she'd just solved the great mystery of life. He lifted her clear of the floor and kissed her with aching tenderness. His happiness was complete, now.

Almost immediately, he began to worry about labor. He remembered when Luis's and Isaac's wives had given birth, and he turned pale.

The doctor patted him on the back. "You'll survive the birth of your children,

Mr. Jacobs, we all do. Yes, even me. I have had to deliver mine. Something, I daresay, you will be spared!"

John laughed with relief, thanked the doctor for his perception, and kissed Ellen again.

She bore him three sons and two daughters in the years that followed, although only two of their children, their son Bass and their daughter Rose Ellen, lived to adulthood. The family grew and prospered in Jacobsville. Later, the entire county, Jacobs, was named for John as well. He diversified his holdings into mining and real estate and banking. He was the first in south Texas to try new techniques in cattle ranching and to use mechanization to improve his land.

The Brown family produced six children in all. Their youngest, Caleb, would move to Chicago and become a famous trial lawyer. His son would be elected to the United States Senate.

The Rodriguez family produced ten children. One of their sons became a Texas Ranger, beginning a family tradition that lived on through subsequent generations.

John Jacobs founded the first bank in Jacobs County, along with the first dry goods store. He worked hard at breeding good cattle, but he made his fortune in the terrible blizzard of 1885–86 in which so many cattlemen lost their shirts. He endowed a college and an orphanage, and, always active in local politics, he was elected to the U.S. Senate at the age of fifty. He and Ellen never parted for fifty years.

His son, Bass Jacobs, married twice. By his young second wife, he had a son, Bass, Jr., and a daughter, Violet Ellen. Bass Jacobs, Jr., was the last of the Jacobs family to own land in Jacobs County. The 3J Ranch was sold after his death. His son, Ty, born in 1955, eventually moved to Arizona and married and settled there. His daughter, Shelby, born in 1961, stayed in Jacobsville and married a local man, Justin Ballenger. They produced three sons. One of them was named John Jackson Jacobs Ballenger, so that the founding father of Shelby's family name would live on in memory.

A bronze statue of Big John Jacobs, mounted on one of the Arabian stallions his ranch became famous for, was erected in the town square of Jacobsville just after the first world war.

Portraits of the Rodriguez family and the Brown family are prominently displayed in the Jacobs County Museum, alongside a portrait of Camellia Ellen Jacobs, dressed in an elegant blue gown, but with a shotgun in a fringed sheath at her feet and a twinkle in her blue eyes. All three portraits, which had belonged to Bass Jacobs, Jr., were donated to the museum by Shelby Jacobs Ballenger. In a glass case nearby are a bow and arrow in a beaded rawhide quiver in which also resides a black-and-white photograph of a Comanche warrior with a blond woman and five children, two of whom are also blond. But that is another story . . .

About the Author

Diana Palmer has a gift for telling the most sensual tales with charm and humor. With over 40 million copies of her books in print, Diana Palmer is one of North America's most beloved authors and is considered one of the top ten romance authors in America.

Diana's hobbies include gardening, archaeology, anthropology, iguanas, astronomy and music. She has been married to James Kyle for over twenty-five years, and they have one son.

We hope you have enjoyed this Large Print book. Other Thorndike, Wheeler or Chivers Press Large Print books are available at your library or directly from the publishers.

For more information about current and upcoming titles, please call or write, without obligation, to:

Publisher
Thorndike Press
295 Kennedy Memorial Drive
Waterville, ME 04901
Tel. (800) 223-1244

Or visit our Web site at:
www.gale.com/thorndike
www.gale.com/wheeler

OR

Chivers Large Print
published by BBC Audiobooks Ltd
St James House, The Square
Lower Bristol Road
Bath BA2 3SB
England
Tel. +44(0) 800 136919
email: bbcaudiobooks@bbc.co.uk
www.bbcaudiobooks.co.uk

All our Large Print titles are designed for easy reading, and all our books are made to last.